The Author

HIDDEN DESIRE

Catherine Cox

HIDDEN DESIRE

Vanguard Press

VANGUARD PAPERBACK

© Copyright 2025
Catherine Cox
Cover photograph Connor Cox

A CIP catalogue record for this title is available from the British
Library.

ISBN 978-1-83794-084-4

Vanguard Press is an imprint of
Pegasus Elliot Mackenzie Publishers Ltd.
www.pegasuspublishers.com

First Published in 2025
Vanguard Press
Sheraton House Castle Park
Cambridge England
Printed & Bound in Great Britain

Dedication

As always, to Kev, my everlasting love and my amazing children, Tanner, Connor, Kaleigh, Love Cathy. Special thanks to my family and friends for all of your support. I'm so grateful to have all of you in my life. Sincere words coming straight from my heart

Acknowledgements

Thank you so much for the people who respect me as a writer. All your kindness and praise gave me the strength to continue writing my second novel. I would never have been able to do what I love and that is to write. Thank you for all the beautiful compliments.

Chapter 1

Anna Maria sat motionless near her father, Michael Cecola, lying peacefully his is very secluded, private hospital room. He observed his beautiful daughter for the longest time, reaching for her petite and tender hand.

He whispered, 'Anna Maria where is your contagious smile. What is bothering you, my beloved daughter. You look so sad and all lone. Is Antonio treating you with much kindness.'

'Of course, he is daddy. Why do you ask?'

'A father knows their children well and, Anna Maria, you are fighting pain deep in your heart. Please tell me what is wrong. I'm here for you. You are my one and only precious baby girl.'

'Daddy, I'm no longer a baby girl. I'm a grown woman.'

'Anna Maria, you will always be my baby girl. I love you and don't you ever forget. I have raised a brilliant and beautiful daughter. You are someone who is very important and well respected by others. You deserve much happiness and wealth. Lately you seem to be in another world, as your deep set and dark eyes tell all. All I have wanted was you to be happy.'

A heavy sigh and within seconds Michael Cecola's tired eyes closed into total darkness. Leaving Anna Maria alone and feeling pain in her cold heart. Her hero is slowly passing. Years ago, she lost her mother and soon also her father. Tears streamed down her chilled cheeks, as she quietly exited his cold hospital room.

Minutes later, she entered through the chapel doors to say a prayer for the man she has always admired, her dear father.

All Anna Maria wanted was to be alone. She sat quietly, nestled in the chapel's pew. Feeling overwhelmed with much guilt and lost words. Fighting back tears in frustration, as she bowed her head forward and then within seconds feeling an unwanted presence breathing down her back.

A deep voice echoed, 'Hey beautiful lady, are you all right?'

Anna Maria sat still. Staring down at her feet she whispered, 'Antonio, please I would like to be alone.'

Without saying a word, he arched forward and gently kissed her neck. Eyeing her closely he proceeded to walk backwards through the chapel doors, moments later exiting.

Anna Maria's mind was pondering with deep thoughts. Thinking of the last time she was truly happy. She smiled, as salty tears streamed down her face. Tears of joy not sorrow. Closing her wet eyes and in her mind, visualizing the most mysterious and gracious man she has ever known, Gunnar McKay. Oh, how Anna Maria loves him and with all her heart. She deeply wishes he would reappear, but for now she must pray and dream that he will return someday. Still fresh in her mind, she remembers the smell of his cologne and sweet taste of bubbling champagne on his tender lips. His piercing blues eyes would paralyze her mind, as her petite body would slowly melt with much anxiety. Suddenly she felt as if he were near. In her mind, visualizing his precious smile, as he whispered how much he loves her and one day they shall wed.

She felt her heart pound. A beat she knows well. A soothing and bittersweet pulse. Minutes later her heart hurt, as Gunnar's beautiful face disappeared back into darkness. Leaving her once again just having a vivid imagination of the man who only exists now in her cold mind. At one time a beautiful fairy tale romance and now an open ending that shall no longer rest. Leaving only a letter and never saying why.

She rested her cold hand in her sweater pocket, gripping a small envelope. Moments later, she entered her father's room. Slowly and painfully unsealing Gunnar's last goodbye letter.

The note read

Anna Maria, I love you deeply
Please forgive me someday. You deserve better.
Love Gunnar.

She just could not understand why. Their relationship was beautiful. What went wrong.

She felt like crying, but there were no more tears to shed. It has been a year since she last saw him. Not a day goes by without beautiful visions of Gunnar exploding in her head. It is hard for Anna Maria to wake up every day. Knowing there will never be another man she will ever love. She knows though to be strong for her dying father and believes she has the will to run one of the most powerful companies in the Midwest.

Breathing deeply, Michael Cecola opens his eyes. He speaks softly, 'Anna Maria, are you here?'

'Yes daddy, of course.'

'Darling have you been crying.'

She replied openly, 'I'm feeling a little under the weather and I'm chilled.'

'Go home, Anna Maria, and have Rosie cook you up something warm. You need to take care of yourself. You look like you have lost weight.'

'Please do not worry about me daddy. I will be fine.'

He smiled at his beautiful daughter. Whispering, 'I love you baby girl and will miss you.',

She could no longer speak, for fear of losing control.

Antonio watched Michael Cecola and Anna Maria intensively for the longest time before tapping on the hospital door. Seconds later he entered in a pompous way. Kissing Anna Maria on her cheek and charming his way towards her father. Smiling, reaching for Mr. Cecola's aching hand.

A smiled appeared on Mr. Cecola's aging face.

Antonic winked and smirked in a cunning way.

Anna Maria sat, unsettled, wanting to release her anger but kept her composure. She has always disliked the way Antonio sucked up to her father. She is convinced he is a clown in disguise. Trying to fool people with his gentlemanly charm and walking away, as if he had won an outstanding award. Lately she has not been impressed by him, as he walks around arrogantly and pretends to be a brilliant businessman. Believing he could persuade and charm everyone including her multimillionaire father. One of the most powerful businessmen in the country. She has witnessed from closed doors his disturbing behavior, continuous lies and believes deep in her heart Antonio could never run her father's company. She believes in six months Cecola & Gold will collapse if Antonio has any part of it. Pretending he travels to do business, instead escapes to the Maya Riviera monthly. He arrives back into the United States carrying imported wines, Cuban cigars and full of gems. Money is all Antonio wants. Somehow and in some way he smoothed his way into Michael Cecola's arms.

Anna Maria is a smart woman. She learned it all from the best, her father. Now she knows what she has to do. Free herself from Antonio and convince her father in some way he is crooked and a thief. She knows it will not be easy. Time is running out. For now, she must be true to Antonio. Please her father and honor his dying wish before it is too late.

'You know, Mr. Cecola,' Antonio said with such honesty in his scratchy voice. 'You are a father I never had.'

Anna Maria rolled her eyes and sighed under her breath. Thinking to herself, why couldn't her father have loved Gunnar the way he adores Antonio. She does not understand. Her father never even met Gunnar and wanted nothing to do with him. It is not fair!

Michael Cecola slowly moved his head facing Anna Maria. Smiling and eyeing her with his dying eyes. He reached for her hand. Speaking softly, 'You are going to be a beautiful bride someday. Antonio will be a good husband. He will take care of you and treat you the way a woman should be treated. You will have it all. No need for you to work. Have your lady lunches Anna Maria and spend days at the spa. You deserve happiness. Enjoy your fortune, for I did this for you. May you be true and be happy until eternity, just like me.'

Fighting for dry eyes, Anna Maria kissed her father's forehead and slowly walked away. Crying hard in the inside and screaming in pain. Facing a steamy window and biting her lower lip. Wanting so badly to jump and rewind back to the future. Not the present and not with Antonio.

Her eyes were swelling with tears and filled with total darkness. A dark world seems to exist, and she feels, as if she is the only one living on Earth. A world she no longer wants to live in, only by Gunnar's side. For now, she only has a dream. The man she truly loves secretly left in the midst of the night. Never saying a word and never again returning. She feels like she has no choice, but to honor her father and his very own wish and that is to marry Antonio Maggiano.

Antonio studied Anna Maria deeply. Wondering what was playing in her head. Knowing to shake his thoughts of negativity and concentrate on more important issues. Like focusing once again on Cecola & Gold and poor Mr. Cecola. Eyeing him from his side, he looked, as if he were already put to rest, from his tired features, to his teary eyes.

Antonio visualized in his mind. Imagining what Michael Cecola would look like, as he lay still and dead in the Cecola Mausoleum. He prays his life ends soon, for he would have everything a man could ever imagine. Owner of Cecola & Gold, which is worth millions. A beautiful bride and a bank account that would never deplete. Only in his dreams could he ever imagine falling into such a wealthy family. Now his dreams are about to come true. He prays Anna Maria will honor her father's wish, as they both make a vow and unite as one in marriage.

'I really think your father needs some rest,' Antonio said in such a sincere way. 'Please, Anna Maria, we shall go.'

'I need more time with my father,' Anna Maria responded harshly. 'He needs to feel loved not betrayed. I like to be alone with him for a few more minutes. Please Antonio let me be.'

Something was up with Anna Maria. Antonio could sense it. Not quite understanding her in the last few weeks.

Could it be because her father is passing soon or is it because she does not want him around.

A great relief of stress triggered from Anna Maria's nerves, as Antonio departed the room. She felt relaxed and warm near her dearest father. Watching him breath heavy and feeling his miserable pain. She so deeply wanted to switch places with him. So, she would not have to live a lie and marry a man she does not even love.

Sitting still and staring into space, she felt numb. Visualizing in her mind how one man made her feel so incredibly sexy and happy. She would wake up smiling every morning feeling wanted and desirable. Now she feels, as if the whole world is crashing down on her.

Life is not always fair, but she seriously knows to get a grip of herself and be strong, before her life really ends in one big tragedy.

Michael Cecola spoke wearily, 'Baby girl, you make me sad. You should be delightful. Life has always been bittersweet for you. I have given you everything you ever wanted and even more. Money brings happiness, not sorrow.'

Thinking quietly in her mind. Anna Maria wished money could buy everything, including happiness. Fortunately, it does not. Money can't buy love, for Gunnar disappeared without a trace. She believes not even a million dollars would bring him back into her arms.

Gunnar knew much about the Cecola family and how powerful they really are. It seemed like every time he picked up the newspaper, one of the Cecola family's face was snapped on the front page. He never did see Anna Maria's face, for she wanted silence and much space. It is as if she never did exist. A smart woman who seemed to always secretly escape the press.

For years the Cecola family seemed to own the windy city. Building impressive skyscrapers and owning the largest chains of elite hotels. In the last year. The Cecola name has been quiet. Quiet in a way, as if Michael Cecola had already passed. As if he were already peacefully lying in a beautiful coffin, made especially for him. Having his favorite flower, the red rose, placed near his heart.

The media seems to be shying away from the Cecola family. Till the day one family member unseals their closed lips and speaks. Being brave and explaining to all how Michael Cecola passed away. Fighting to survive each day and in the end not winning the battle. He was weak and fought long and hard. His tired eyes closed into darkness.

Anna Maria is dreading the day when her father's eyes remain shut. Preparing a second funeral for the one she loves. Being escorted by police and sitting in the front pew of St. Mary's Cathedral church. Listening to readings and speeches. Wanting it to be all over, before it had begun.

It was hard enough when Anna Maria lost her mother and now soon to be her father. There will be no one for her to hold or love.

Bending slightly forward she gently kissed her father's chilled cheek. She softly whispered with tears in her eyes, 'Daddy, I love you. You have always been my hero. Rest now I'll be back soon.'

Michael Cecola half smiled, 'Beautiful girl, I love you.' He then closed his tired eyes.

She stood still, staring at her father for the longest time. Closing her eyes and remembering what he looked like when he was well. His dark puppy eyes said all, from his kindness to loving life and a gigantic smile that would never end.

She does feel blessed to have grown up with such an extraordinary father. Anna Maria feels, as if life can be bittersweet in the end, life can take you away by surprise.

Soon her father will no longer feel pain, for his guardian angel will miraculously eat his cancer away and sail his spirit up into a new and peaceful world. A world we are afraid of, but a beautiful heaven full of love, solitude and tranquility.

Chapter 2

Loud thunder and cracks of lightning seem to be exploding in every direction causing Anna Maria to fall to her knees. She could feel the windows vibrate. The building swaying back and forth, sending chills down her spine. She has always been fascinated and intrigued by spring storms never fearing Mother Nature and her ability to create such madness. Learning to understand the atmosphere and such power Mother Nature brings to Earth. Only having one fear and never releasing her sealed lips to others about her deep secret. She has a disturbing fear and a very powerful one, the fear of heights.

Entering every morning through the Cecola & Gold doors, she would stand face to face in front of the glass mirrors. Inching her way towards the elevator door and stepping inside, feeling a great rush of panic and anxiety tear through her fearful body. Facing the floor, as she becomes lightheaded and pains of nauseas grumbles in her inside. Closing her eyes and holding her breath, until her roller coaster ride comes to a complete end. Inhaling deeply and releasing her uncontrollable fear and panic. Walking away feeling numb and overwhelmed with having such a phobia. She enters once again through the elevator door leading to her father's office on the thirty-fourth floor, free and feeling very much alive.

The only time she fears wicked and uncontrollable storms is when she is in her father's high rise, above the mystical clouds. Always having this fear and hiding it as long she could remember. How she fears heights, to the point where she feels as if she will pass out. Having a difficult time concentrating and keeping her strength up.

Anna Maria was not even aware a wicked storm was moving through the city. She cautiously glimpsed through the foggy glass windows starring at the mysterious water before closing the blinds.

Lake Michigan was dark and eerie, as if an unwanted creature was lurking among the deep and blackened water. Swelling with enormous waves, as they came crashing against hundreds of boats. Many seem to be sinking while others disappeared among the stormy waters. Beautiful sail boats tangling in their own sails. Owners were desperately trying to retrieve their pride and joy. They had no luck knowing to return when the strong winds have slowly diminished.

Anna Maria visualized Gunnar in her mind. Remembering as if it were yesterday. When Gunnar and she sailed his sailboat straight into a vicious summer storm. One sail collided right into her hip sending her body straight into the blustering waters. She has loved the fresh waters since she was a little girl. Learning to swim at a very young age and never having a fear of drowning. Only the creatures living underneath the dark waters frightened her. She swam fast and was able to climb back into the boat without any distress. Collapsing into his arms and feeling blessed to have survived. Loving a man who gave her strength and the meaning of life.

Peeking through the window for the last time, she smiled closing the remaining blind and feeling an overwhelming presence, as if Gunnar were two feet away. She inhaled deeply not knowing quite at that very moment what to do.

Piercing loud thunder amplified the room, as if a bomb went off. The lights were flickering on and off causing her to panic. Her whole life she has been dreading this day. Being numerous stories above ground and not able to see to leave the building. Thunder was crashing from every angle of the building. Feeling alone and in a great whirlwind of panic. From the corner of her eye. She saw a bright flash from the murky skies piercing through the window and striking inches from her. Seconds later the whole building went black.

Breathing deeply with much anxiety, Anna Maria slowly stood up. Fighting back her fears and praying for someone's help. She closely eyed a flickering light which seemed to be streaming from the main doors. Desperately trying to be calm and wanting so badly to be rescued. The lights were fading in and out still moving in the same direction towards her. No words were spoken, as she stood frozen in total fear. Shaking like a leaf. She slowly arched up, as she nervously faced the main entrance. One light at a time seem to flicker on and off. Causing her vision to become blurred. A shadow appeared in the distance. She could not quite make out who was approaching, as once again the room turned black as night. Much tension pulsed through her body. She wanted to run and hide but there was no place to go. Darkness filled the room. Anna Maria's heart was beating faster and faster, as her eyes were glued towards the shadowy figure pulsing lights were all around the room. A silhouette of Gunnar appeared and then vanished back into darkness. Was Anna Maria hallucinating? She grew nervous and an image of Antonio reflected in front of her straining eyes. Was this all an illusion of Anna Maria's mind playing tricks on her? She badly wanted to speak, but there were no words releasing from her sealed lips.

A deep voice spoke, 'Anna Maria is that you?'

Standing in total darkness. Anna Maria grew alarmed and a mirage of lights twinkled, as if it was the 4th of July. Fading in and out and again the room went black Thunder erupted from the corner of the room and then a flash of lightening. Penetrating a glow and an image of Gunnar once again appeared.

She smiled as tears streamed from her blurry eyes. Was Gunnar really standing in front of her or an image. Anna Maria became peaceful. His stunning handsome face was inches away. She could tell from the smell of his cologne to his deep dark blue eyes. They were as beautiful as the deep blue sea.

Gunnar smiled.

The room was no longer black, but bright as the morning sky. All lights had reappeared, as if Gunnar had planned his grand entrance.

She swallowed hard not believing her eyes. Not only was Gunnar standing proud, but Antonio by his side.

Gunnar's eye met Anna Maria's. They became glued not releasing their sealed lips and taking it all in. She deeply wanted to cry and reach for the man she has always loved. Instead, Antonio ran into her arms. Holding tightly and speaking softly. Oh, my love I'm so glad you are all right.

Anna Maria pulled away never leaving sight of Gunnar.

There has never been chemistry between her and Antonio. He so badly wanted to deny it but struggling hard to hold on.

Anna Maria closed her eyes. Praying Gunnar was not an illusion, but her knight in shining armor. Rescuing her and taking her far away to a beautiful place full of laughter and love. Hidden and secluded far away.

Slowing opening her eyes. She smiled, as peace and hope ran through her body. Gunnar was inches away. Grinning and winking in away, as if no words should be spoken. Cherishing the moment, as if there will be no tomorrow. Anna Maria's bulging eyes remained open straining from blinking for fear Gunnar would once again just disappear.

'Anna Maria, answer me,' Antonio demanded.

Still facing Gunnar, she paused. Moments later she quietly spoke, 'Of course I'm fine.' Shaking away her tensed nerves and breathing deeply, as she slowly walked towards the window.

Antonio spoke it seems as if the storm is slowly moving away. The power is on and I need to make a call. He then without any hesitation stormed through the double doors leading towards the end of the hall. Leaving Gunnar alone and having Anna Maria only inches away from his side.

When Antonio's shadow was clearly invisible. Gunnar lunched forward swallowing Anna Maria into his arms. His whispered I have always loved you. Please do forgive me. We will talk later, for now pretend I do not even exist.

The sound of his voice frightened her, as she gripped his shirt tightly not wanting to let go. Beneath his tailored shirt. She could feel the stretching of his dense muscles and warmth of his heart. Her body ached with emptiness and wanted his tender touch to last to eternity.

His fingertips slowly caressed down her spine. Leaving her helpless and melting for his passion. Running his right hand through her long hair and passionately kissing her slender neck.

He whispered, 'Anna Maria, I love you.' Moving his mouth towards her round lips and teasing her with his smoky dark blue eyes. His voice was deep and thick.

Salty tears strung down her face, as Gunnar gently wiped them away.

He smiled, 'God, you make me crazy. Forgive me.'
He swiftly dipped his head and forcefully kissed her
mouth. His intensity pierced her, leaving her mind
spinning. Anna Maria's heart ached and eyes watered full
of pain and desire.

Pulling away, Gunnar smiled, as he saw the pain in
her teary eyes.

One minute she was kissing the man who stole her
heart and ran away with it. Now feeling unsure about why
he has come back and with Antonio near his side. She
looked up at him. Wondering how she would be able to get
the words out. Why she could never see him again.

The double doors swung open, as if another blackout
reappeared. Antonio looked distressed. He spoke, 'I'm so
sorry I apologize. Gunnar I would like to introduce you to
my fiancé. This is my beautiful bride to be Anna Maria
Cecola.'

Stepping forward, Gunnar grinned. Reaching for
Anna Maria' petite hand and gently holding it, as if this
was their first hello and again another last goodbye.

He spoke with a rich and deep voice. 'It certainly is
a pleasure to meet you.' Still gazing into her hurtful eye
and feeling overwhelmed by her stunning presence.

Anna Maria swallowed hard, nervously smiling and
eyeing him in a way like no other. She kindly spoke,
'Thank you,' bowing her head forward and then releasing
his muscular hand.

Looking at Anna Maria, Antonio could sense she was disturbed. Moving towards her and feeling not wanted, as she faced the other way.

Well I found an outstanding architect. He will design our next hotel located in the heart of the city.

Eyeing Antonio, Anna Maria inhaled deeply, 'Who must that be?' Wanting to scream and push him thirty-four stories to the ground. Where he came from and in a coning way smoothed talked his way to the top. Taking over her prime position, because of her father's dying wish. She could only pray now and hope her father holds on a little longer.

Antonio spoke in an arrogant way. Gunnar McKay now works for Cecola & Gold.

,Excuse me?' Anna Maria said. 'What right do you have in hiring?'

'I have all the right in the world to hire who I want.'

Hot blood was rushing deeply though her pulsing veins. She felt anger and yet a feverish desire for Gunnar's presence. Not knowing quite what was up his sleeve? Why would he want to work for Cecola & Gold? Did Antonio seek him out or did Gunnar want to be hired. Persuading and charming his clever ways right into Antonio's games. Hopefully this was not a game Gunnar wanted to play, for fear he will lose in the end. He should know better to never play hard ball with a family who is so powerful and can be extremely ruthless.

'Anna Maria. Please' Antonio said. 'You will love his work.'

She vocalized harshly, 'This is not the point. I would like you to confide in me before you decide on a big decision like this one. You are not in charge!'

Still standing with much dignity Gunnar's eyes welled up. Believing now there is still hope between him and Anna Maria. Sensing there was never any platonic love between them. Smiling in the inside and breathing calmly. Expressing a slight grin and winking at Anna Maria in a sly way. Never leaving sight of her irresistible body.

Gunnar hesitated, 'Excuse me, should I leave you two alone to discuss this.'

In her mind, Anna Maria never wanted to lose sight of his beautiful vision ever again.

Knowing though there will never be a Cinderella love story between them now or in the future.

Antonio demanded, 'No, you are not going anywhere! Follow me and I will show you to your new office. You will love it. The view is spectacular facing Oak Street beach.'

Trailing behind Antonio, Gunnar looked like a lost puppy. So deeply wanting to grab Anna Maria into his arms and tell her the truth. How he abandoned the only woman he has ever loved and fighting like hell to get her back.

How could this all be happening? Why Gunnar are you back? Visions of his beautiful face continue to play in her mind like a broken record player skipping from the beginning to the end. Anna Maria collapsed her face into her sweaty palms, crying again. If it is not tears shedding for her dying father, it is tears of joy and pain from the man who has always given her great pleasure. Pleasure of living and pleasure in bed. Her mind was racing with beautiful thoughts and fond memories. Oh, how she adores Gunnar from his unforgettable way to his magical touch. Caressing her in a way that is so seductive and mystifying. Pulsing her body in magical ways, as she becomes limp and tireless.

Standing alone for the longest time and breathing in a scent. A scent she knows well. Breathing deeper, as his unforgettable rich aroma lingers all around her. Masculine like she has always remembered. Closing her eyes and inhaling deeply. Remembering how at one time their platonic love exploded with passion and undeniable desire. Relaxing and feeling as if Gunnar were caressing her gentle body. Quivering and imagining his body penetrating her. Loving and never forgetting such an incredible sensation. Thinking more and more about Gunnar and his wildness made her extremely bothered. Bothered in a way that he secretly escaped and now works inches away. Breathing deeper, Anna Maria felt aroused just thinking about one man who gave her great pleasure and seductiveness. How could she not want to be inches from him? His tender kiss and kind words of sorrow tells all. He really is sorry but why did he leave and for one year and now works for her father's company.

Overwhelmed and exhausted but feeling exhilarated. Anna Maria's mind was racing with deep and triggering thoughts. Thinking quietly and wondering if her life will ever be simple. She knows once her father passes, she will need someone to hold and help her through such a horrible ordeal. Blurring with fresh tears she caught a glimpse of Gunnar from the corner of her eye. Arching away and staring downward not wanting him to see her inner pain.

Gazing at his once beautiful woman, Gunnar senses much pain. Realizing deep down he created Anna Maria's sorrows. Her dramatic and dark eyes seem to be hiding something inside. A secret only she knows and will never tell. No more glitter in her once prominent eyes and her forever smile lies still. Staring intensively, Gunnar felt strongly in unsealing Anna Maria's secured lips from a secret which is deep and haunting. May he also speak of the truth. A horrifying deep secret of his disappearance.

Will Anna Maria ever forgive? He was not sure but, will fight like hell to convince her he was weak and truly wrong. How will the right words release from his sealed lips without causing tremendous pain. Will she believe him or her precious father?

Chapter 3

Lying alone in bed, Anna Maria cried until there were no more tears to be shed. Alone and lonely again feeling ashamed. Day after day pretending to be someone she is not. Living a life for others marrying an ungrateful man just to please her father. Why must her father be so difficult? Will he ever forgive her if she does not marry Antonio? Will her father's spirit haunt her daily above the gates of Heaven or will he peacefully sail away causing no friction or bitterness?

Smiling as Gunnar's beautiful complexion appears in her vivid mind. Closing her eyes and breathing calmly, as if he were near. Feeling excited like a child and never wanting to shed her emotions. A wonderful sensation and one she will never forget.

A tapping noise startled her, sending her to her feet. She noticed how the curtains were swaying from the light breeze. Wondering in her mind if she should remain still or calmly walk towards the open window.

A soft voice spoke, 'Anna Maria.'

Swallowing hard and breathing heavy she stood frozen

Again, the gently and harsh voice spoke, 'Anna Maria, I cannot hold on any longer. Please help me.'

Smiling and remembering old times, as if it were yesterday. Secretly Gunnar would climb the trellis leading to her bedroom. No one ever found out, even her father's bodyguards never knew.

Anna Maria whispered, 'Gunnar are you crazy? What on earth are you doing?'

'Oh, just hanging.'

Laughing and amused Anna Maria chuckled, 'Just hanging are you. Well maybe you should keep hanging. You vanished and left me hanging for a year and still I do not know why. Why did you leave me Gunnar?'

Fresh tears welled up in her eyes.

Struggling to hold on, Gunnar inhaled deeply. 'Please, Anna Maria, just help me and I will tell you everything.'

'Everything?' Anna Maria said.

'Everything, now please.' Gunnar insisted.

Smiling, Anna Maria spoke, 'After I count to three. Use all your strength and arch forward.'

Holding tight against Gunnar's collar Anna Maria helped pull his muscular body through the window, as he landed on her petite body. Facing her tiny breast and grinning he arched up and softly whispered you still have the most beautiful round shape breast I have ever seen.

Face to face they both smiled. Eyeing each other and feeling their bodies pulse as one. No movement and no words were spoken for the longest time.

Gunnar winked, 'I love you. Please forgive me.'

Salty tears streamed down her chilled cheeks. She cried, 'Why Gunnar, why? Why did you leave me? What did I do wrong?'

Gunnar whispered, 'Anna Maria, I had no choice.' Wrapping his arm around her tender body and gently squeezing. Saying quietly, 'I have always loved you. I loved you the first moment I laid eyes on you. You are genuine and the most beautiful woman I have ever known. You make me crazy with your dazzling long black hair and dramatic dark eyes. You are confident and your energy level never ends. I need you and I have missed you tremendously.'

Anna Maria felt her body become limp and light. Not ever wanting to release his irresistible body and feeling the warmth of his muscles penetrating against her breast. Feeling excited, as if this was the first time they have ever made love. In her mind she has dreamed of this day for a very long time. Praying Gunnar would return and feel peace with herself once again.

He lifted her off the floor and gentle placed her in the center of the bed. Smiling and smelling a scent of a beautiful woman. A perfume he knows well. An arousing scent and one he had deeply missed. His passion for her flared again. Flexed muscles and heated veins. Aroused and stimulated by her tender and slender body. Removing her satin top and discarding his clothes.

He kissed her round lips down to her tiny breast. Caressing softly with a gentle touch. Loving the silky smoothness of her skin. It gleamed with a pearl white finish. He could clearly see her. The lean legs, small protruding breast and slender neck. She was feminine and beautiful in every way.

Gliding his hands, as if they were a soft feather and taunting her with exhilarating affection. Tracing her small curves and filling his hands with her breast. His thumbs sliding over her nipples arousing and teasing endlessly. Demonstrating his affection and alluring in slowly.

Her breathing grew rapidly. Reaching out provocatively touching him, whispering, 'I love you.' Melting in his arms with excitement. Closing her wet eyes and smiling. She lay openly and calmly feeling as if she were a woman again.

Gunnar whispered, 'Anna Maria, you make me crazy'. He continuously kissed her ear lobe and her slender neck. Engulfing her lips and slithering his tongue into her wet mouth pressing deeply. Caressing one hand against her tiny breast and moving his other hand down her slender leg. Moving slowly and sliding his muscular hand between her moist inner thighs. Removing the rest of his clothes gliding his fingers against her hips, around her breast and again back to the inner thighs.

She was speechless winding her arms around his muscular shoulders. Lifting her face to be kissed feeling aroused and feverish. Her body was melting with much anxiety.

His magical fingers deepened through her inner thighs. Pressing and sliding. He moved with her tempo drawing her lips against his, applying heaviness and releasing. Moving towards her chest and inhaling her nipples deep in his mouth licking and relieving them.

He had this way of teasing her until the point of climax and then releasing his fingers. Loving the way, he made her feel and watching her body collapse. Giving her much pleasure and teasing her until she could take no more. She welcomed his tender touch driving his excitement level even higher. He moved his body between her thighs kissing and licking his way inside. Shifting her legs outward moving his mouth on her most pleasurable area. Wanting to give her ultimate pleasure. She smiled moaned and arched upward. Enjoying his tender licks and the caressing of his fingers. Leaving her melting body weak and desirable. Craving for his fierce energy. Her hands tucking at his shoulder blades wanting him inside of her. He did not want to stop but wanted the ultimate climax. Eyeing him in a seductive way she gleamed. 'I want you Gunnar McKay.' Her hands pulled behind his shoulder blades forcing him to lead the way. He knew what she ultimately wanted, climax as one. He slowly arched forward entering and passively covering her helpless body. Hearing her moan of great satisfaction. Penetrating deeper listening to her sweet aches of delight. Holding strong, kissing her tender mouth. Asking her when to release and explode. Needing her to response. He was near. His tongue danced in her mouth moving tenderly with a sexy rhythm. She was near. He could tell. She arched up locking her thighs moving fierce against his masculine frame. It was fantastic! More than fantastic. It was exhilarating. Feeling her warm dizzy body dance. Her legs hugged, wrapped around his chiseled center giving her wanted pleasure.

To Gunnar it was so powerful embracing so intimately with Anna Maria. Feeling welcomed once again wanting her so deeply and knowing she never stopped loving him.

Penetrating deeper, Gunnar released knowing seconds before she had already climaxed to the fullest. Bursting a moan penetrating with each beat, releasing tension cherishing the moment.

Gunnar was high on life and once it was over gathering her into his moist arms. Holding her close he knew she was happy from the sweet beats of her warm heart. He knew what happiness was. This extraordinary woman holding her and feeling her passionate love.

One year has passed. He deserted a passionate and brilliant woman. How will he ever repay her for his internal misery? Seeing the pain, he had caused in her dominant eyes, fragile body and somber ways. Time will tell. Heal her inner pain and forgive him for fleeing without a trace.

Lying still, admiring her beauty as she peacefully sleeps. Curled like a ball facing him with no expression. Just still as the night. Beautiful and gentle like the morning breeze. Caressing lightly against her blush cheek, as if he had a light feather stroking gently and motionlessly. Taking it all in, admiring her beautiful face and elegant body. Blessed to have her near his side grinning, breathing and standing proud. For he believes he has won his beautiful lady back. Bending forward he whispered I love you

She smiled while she slept.

He watched her deeply. Luscious lips, fresh white tip nails, glowing skin. A beautiful princess to be rescued.

Turning away never looking back. One night of endless pleasures. A new beginning filled with hopes and dreams. One fairy tale romance. Lasting till eternity and continuing above the golden gates of heaven.

Chapter 4

The minutes ticked by. Eyeing the clock. Every second was excruciating. Wondering in her mind if today would be the day her father's painful eyes remain secure and quiet. She paced back and forth near his side. Glancing down at her watch. Time was critical not wanting him to say his final goodbye. He must know the truth. The love in her life and endless hours of painful sorrow. Will he forgive her or turn in the opposite direction cursing underneath his breath

A raspy voice startled her, she smiled

Whispering softly Mr. Cecola spoke brokenly. 'You are gleaming today my beautiful girl. You light up the room with your dark and sparking eyes. Why the change? Fresh new you poised with such confidence. I have deeply missed the light of fire in your brilliant eyes. Is my Anna Maria back?'

Smiling delightfully standing proud and sending her father a message through her warm and glowing appearance. She could tell her father's mind was racing with deep thoughts. He badly wanted to speak but was having a difficult time releasing words from his closed mouth. His pain had worsened causing much difficulty in speaking.

She held tight to his hand. Eyeing him and crying in the inside for his miserable pain. Seeing him in such distress made her suddenly heart-sick. Suffering in such agony and nothing she could do to stop his dreadful misery. Only her comfort and warm heart seems to keep him surviving day to day.

She must tell. Rehearsing in her mind like a broken record, from the beginning to the end. Believing he will have faith to honor her wish. She whispered leaning over his body.' Daddy I need to tell you something that is very important. Are you awake?'

No movement response or blinking.' Please Daddy, are you there?'

Minutes dragged by, not an echo was heard in the room

Bending down she tenderly kissed his forehead. Saying, 'Daddy, I hope you can forgive me turning away and existing. Praying her dreams do come true.

He slightly opened one eye. Watching his beautiful daughter gracefully depart from his side. He deeply loves her more than words could say. His princess and only daughter.

In his cold and painful mind. He could sense Anna Maria's warm heart. A new woman and apparently a new man had arrived in her life. He could tell from the sparkle in her eyes, to the gigantic smile on face that never ended. Till she quietly exited.

He must keep his promise for his beautiful daughter. Not ready to hear her speak. Knowing what hurtful words, he will hear. He must be strong and fight for his belief. Wanting his baby girl to live life as he thinks she should live. Be wealthy and happy.

His heart fluttered skipping faster and faster. Showing distress while being connected to a monitoring machine. He glanced over his shoulder. Staring at the black sketch marks pulsing up and down, erratic patterns.

Michael Cecola inhaled deeply as if feeling his last breath. Relaxing and calmly visualizing his beautiful bride of many years as, she is resting peacefully above the golden gates of heaven. Soon they shall be husband and wife again spiritually. Smiling and feeling as he remains still and as quiet the night. Remembering her young and beautiful. Deeply missing her and will once again be by her side. Not wanting to die and leave his precious daughter behind, but he has another love waiting patiently in a beautiful world called heaven. He slowly smiled and closed his tired eyes back into total darkness.

Chapter 5

A dreadful sickening feeling penetrated Anna Maria's nerves. One she has been holding for a very long time until last night.

Where is Gunnar? The office was cold and empty. No voices, warmth or happy faces. Just painful memories of Gunnar leaving her in the mist of the night.

Could this be true? Did he leave her once again? Feeling empty alone and scared of living without him. Walking around in a daze. Snooping through windows wondering where he was? Fear instilled inside of her tensed body. Leaving her stone cold and extremely nervous. Fresh tears developed rapidly in her grieving eyes. Feeling nausea and panic.

Did Antonio find out about last night?

What did he do to Gunnar?

She paced the room fearing Antonio. Did he tell her father?

Melting her wet eyes into the palm of her hands she cried. Praying Gunnar did not vanish.

Last night was amazing. It was more than amazing. It was just perfect.

How could Gunnar do this to her? She felt something between them. Love ,excitement and the ultimate explosion one couple can create passion.

There was a reason why he left and reappeared

Last night was incredible amazing passionate and undeniable.

He came back for her. She could tell.

What is he hiding? Why has he not told her the truth? Will his words cause pain?

Her mind was wondering with happy and disturbing thoughts. Beautiful memories of Gunnar. Ugly visions of Antonio and his bizarre behavior repeating in her head over and over.

Can she ever trust Gunnar again? Once she knows the truth maybe faith will arise once again

Forehead resting on her desk, arms protruded, eyes closed. Suddenly feeling a presence. Looking up standing proud, Gunnar McKay.

She smiled, 'I thought you—'

'No need to say anything. It is ok. I'm here and believe me I will never ever leave you again.'

Moving forward he gently lifted her chin. Glancing into her deep and rich eyes. Winking, 'I love you,' turning away.

'Damn it, Gunnar,' she shouted! 'You are making me crazy. What on earth are you doing to me? Walking away not saying a word. Eyeing me with a mischievous look in your eyes. I cannot not handle this anymore.'

She sobbed, covering her mouth. Staring to the floor.

Reaching for her arm. She turned away.

He reached out again bracing his arms around her tender body. Forcefully piercing her tiny frame against his tense muscles of his chest.

No resistance.

He spoke, 'Anna Maria give me time.'

'You've had enough time.'

'No,' he demanded! 'Understand one thing. I truly love you.'

No words were spoken. They could read each other's minds. Holding embracing and feeling warmth among their pulsing veins.

Gently kissing her lips, he spoke openly. 'No one will ever come between us again. I promise you,' wiping a fresh tear smiling turning away.

She inhaled deeply feeling excited and forgetting about the bad.

He is a man in every woman's provocative dreams sexy, muscular and irresistible. Spontaneous arrogant in a good way and charming. This is what Anna Maria loves about him. A man every woman would love to wake up to each morning. With his intoxicating piercing blue eyes and luscious lips.

Standing still, closing her eyes and daydreaming. Dreaming of the most precious and gentle man on this earth. Feeling numb as if Gunnar is caressing her skin. A gentle touch, one she has always remembered. Never, even at the worst times, deleting him from her mind

Still visualizing beautiful thoughts. Anna Maria smiled, remembering last night. How it was precious and romantic. Making love and feeling loved. What every woman craves.

Loneliness hurts and puts fear in one's mind. Anna Maria no longer feels the excruciating pain of being alone. She is alive. Letting go of her aching pains and her cold heart. Feeling blessed no more tears to be shed. Healed broken heart and no more dying eyes. All she ever wanted was Gunnar McKay. Her one and only true love. May she see light again. Never ending love story filled with much pleasure and years of yearning each other's desire.

Sitting upright with her hands in a prayer position, she looked upward. Smiling and eyeing the ceiling, as if she saw a precious face. Sealed lips and starry eyes.

She prayed silently,

Please forgive me, for I'm committing a sin. I'm dishonoring my father's dying wish and loving another man. I'm happy again. Please respect my decision. I believe in my faith and want to live life to the fullest. Please I'm, begging you to reach out to my father before it is too late. Convince him he is wrong. Just whisper something.

Amend

Ever since Gunnar returned. Looking more stunning than ever. Anna Maria has been unable to focus and concentrate. A continuous smile rises on her oval face. Blushed cheeks and mystic eyes that shine as bright as the starry sky.

Love is precious and tender.

Looking across the room. He stood firm, proud and strong. His tense muscles flexed and formed evenly underneath his fitted press shirt. Tall, trim and well defined. His eyes calming and deep blue. He is a beautiful man with extraordinary features and a smile that will capture your heart. More beautiful than ever. Soft wrinkles lining the edges of his eyes. Maturing and aging well.

She smiled just thinking about Gunnar. Feeling aroused, protected and seductive. Loving a man who deeply sparks her heart and makes her feel wanted and beautiful.

Wanting to run and hide but, again there was nowhere to be free. Antonio came strutting her way in a pompous way.

She felt sickened, weak and unable to communicate. Turning away and avoiding his devious eyes, no use.

He spoken arrogantly. 'Anna Maria, you look ravishing.'

She felt nauseas. Wondering if he was serious or speaking of another fib.

'No Antonio, this is the first time today we have spoken.'

'Well, you do', gently kissing her cheek, disappearing down the hall, turning towards the elevator.

What was that all about. Still thinking and curiously wondering what he was doing or up to. Feeling alarmed, as if he senses warmth between her and Gunnar.

Paranoid and suspicious, will her life ever be normal?

She must find out the truth even if it shall endanger someone she deeply loves. First, she must talk to her dying father and tell all. Then hear Gunnar's true words of why he deserted her and now mysteriously appears and works for Cecola & Gold.

She inhaled deeply. Why is my life so difficult? Why cannot I be free and love Gunnar? Please someone help me before it is too late.

Chapter 6

Deeply inhaling the fresh crisp air, Anna Maria could easily breathe, feeling relaxed and at home. Feeling her clean and clear lungs. No pollution, just pleasant and easy breathing. Fresh air at last. No fog, haze or disturbance in the atmosphere.

Anna Maria felt more at home hanging out at the cottage then she did anywhere else. Her childhood secret getaway. Hidden miles away, peaceful, paradise, calm and quiet. Except, for the wild lurking in the night. Her special place secluded on a remote and scarce island. In the middle of nowhere, isolated, solitude and a beautiful country to escape and feel no inner pain.

Breathing calmly, she smiled. Relaxing, feeling blessed to have a special hideaway she truly calls home. Being herself and forgetting about the busy life she left behind. No phones, smog, noise and eschewing people.

She sat outside. Looking over the balcony admiring such an extraordinary view. A small and distant lake. Nestled among pine and oak trees. Trees so old and tall. The peaks seem to be touching the sky. All so beautiful and magical.

She grinned with delight, feeling so happy and peaceful. Loving what she sees and taking it all in, as if this was the first sight of paradise.

Fleeing from her hectic life and traveling hours to reach her destination. Her secluded cottage and one she truly loves.

Facing the calm waters, she smiled. Remembering weekends, as if she were a child again. Now all grown up with vivid and fond memories.

The only thing missing now in her life and at her very own sanctuary is Gunnar McKay. Oh, how she wished he were near and capturing all the beauty which surrounds her

In the past, she would secretly escape to the cottage with Gunnar and fall in love all over again, as they would make passionate love for hours. Pretending they were the one and only who exist. Exiting outdoor, breathing the scent of the dense woods and then capturing every moment, as if there would never be another tomorrow.

Allowing the gentle breeze to sail them along the mysterious lake, sailing for hours and capturing a dramatic world that only a few people have ever cherished. The great outdoors, fresh and open waters filled with mysterious creatures. The outer perimeter of the hidden lake is surrounded by the wild eyeing them, as if they were invading their territory. A beautiful place filled with silence, peace and fond memories.

Anna Maria has magical and beautiful memories, even more monumental as years have passed. Having Gunnar near her side and engulfing a hidden world, only a few have fathomed. One she truly respects and can relate to day to day.

Visualizing in her mind. She could clearly see her father's cold eyes, filled with hate and despair. Burning with deep hot emotions. His pulse triggered, heartbeat raced, leaving her frantically ill.

Rehearsing in her mind for hours, how she would communicate with her father and tell him the truth. The truth was told, knowing he had heard it all, from the beginning to the end. Anna Maria whispered passionately in her father's ear. Speaking honestly and truthfully.

Pleading for forgiveness and to disobey his dying wish, for she is happy and very much in love.

His glaring eyes said all, disappointment, anger and above all, full of fire. He did not twitch an inch just heated vibes penetrating through his bulging veins trailing down his weathered neck. Haunting words he desperately did not want to hear. He closed his eyes into darkness, with no smile, praise, words spoken, just a goodbye, until Anna Maria comes to her senses.

She cried for hours, knowing her father heard every word she had said. Telling him openly Antonio is not the man she loves. She could not bring herself to speak ugly about him. She knew to give it time. One day at a time. Realizing now talking the truth to her father was not going to be easy at all. He is stubborn as an ox and very bull headed. A grown man who does not give up until he gets whatever he wants, no matter if he hurts someone he loves or despises.

Pacing the hospital room, Anna Maria stood proud and strong. Speaking of one man who loves her deeply and brings much happiness. Speaking honestly and communicating, in a way as never before. Mr. Cecola is a man who shows no emotions. He is pig headed and has never lost.

Anna Maria rested on her hands and knees, pleading for her father to let go and move on. Give his strength to her and end this game he must play. She spoke harshly, I'm your daughter. You have always said to be happy. Well, I have been miserable and depressed for nearly a year now. Dying on the inside and crying daily. Not wanting to live any longer. Closing her eyes, following a light and find mother resting peacefully.

She sobbed, 'Yes, Daddy, I wanted to be by my mom like I was a little girl. She always gave me comfort and love. Telling me how pretty and sweet I am. I miss Mom. I need someone and found a man I want to be with for the rest of my life. I'm truly happy once again. Mom would be proud of me. She always gave me the strength to move forward, never making me feel bad and appreciating me as who I am.'

Crying even harder, she gasped for air. 'Why did Mom have to leave? I miss her and loved her so much. She was so beautiful. Why did the Lord take her from us? She was always there for me.'

Minutes went by. She just cried. In her mind. Pinpointing words to release from her chilled lips, until she had the strength to speak again.

Catching her breath and inhaling deeply, she spoke somberly, 'Daddy, your time is almost up. I will be all alone. Living a life of hell, because I do not love Antonio. He is an arrogant and pompous asshole. I become weak and ill whenever he is near. Is this how you want me to live? Do you want me to follow you up in Heaven relatively soon, because believe I will die and so will Cecola & Gold?'

She vocalized sharply, 'You know damn well I can run Cecola & Gold. You just cannot handle a woman in the work field. You are old fashioned and will never change. Well, Daddy I'm grown up and deserve love and happiness.'

She slowly moved towards his side. She said, 'You can believe what you want to. I'm in love. I have loved this wonderful man for a very long time. No one will ever break us apart again. You are not going to stop me this time. I will fight like hell. I'm leaving, Daddy, and will not be back for a long time.'

She walked away frustrated, teary eyed and so sad, sad for her father and sad for herself. Glancing lightly behind her shoulder and witnessing tears stream down her father's pale face. No movement just still as the night with his eyes deeply shut.

This was the very first time Anna Maria has ever stood up to her father. She was scared, exhausted and above all feeling rather proud of herself.

Glancing to the sky and smiling. Knowing her mother heard and saw all. In her mind, Anna Maria could clearly see her mother's tender wink and precious princess wave. Cheering her on and clapping, as if she had won the gold.

Minutes later, Anna Maria returned to her father's peaceful room. Not saying a word, gently kissing his cold cheek, whispering, 'I love you please forgive me. Daddy you truly are my hero and do not ever forget. You taught me to be strong and courageous. Please don't be mad.'

She exited the double doors. She smiled.

Wiping fresh tears from her cheeks, Anna Maria sat on the balcony daydreaming about her feud with her father and romanticising with Gunnar.

Sipping white wine from her chilled glass she shivered. Never forgetting how the crisp air felt in the great woods and the smell of fresh pine. Taking in all the beauty and how quiet earth seemed miles away from the city.an enchanting feeling, one she has desperately missed. Wondering now why she took so long to come back to a place she feels much alive and at home.

Looking at her empty glass, feeling alone, but loving where she is and admiring all the beauty that surrounds her. She looked in every direction, seeing miles of wilderness, fresh waters and curious eyes of the wild. Following her every move. Staying hidden, until night falls and then edging further away from their hidden boundaries.

Being alone in the great woods never frightened Anna Maria. She felt at peace, except at night when the animals roam and feast on their prey. Taking her many years to accept the wild, no longer alarmed and sensing an eeriness feeling in the quiet night. She watched the sun slowly diminish, as it inched its way down the rough terrain. Noticing from the distance the sky was still rather bright. Silhouettes of flickering stars foaming and a bright moon. One that seemed so near, as if you could reach out and gentle touch. Evenings like this one she has always remembered beautiful, settling, quiet, still and so breathtaking.

Moving inside and eyeing all the beauty from her balcony window facing the east. Feeling tired and worn out. She decided to call it a night. She laid peacefully on her overly large king size bed, much too big for just one person. Moving from side to side, fluffing her pillows and patiently trying to fall asleep.

Her mind was racing with disturbing thoughts of her father. Praying he does not have his final breath of air this evening. Wanting him desperately to hold on. Hoping her strong words expressed yesterday will sink in and give him more time to think. Thinking maybe it was not such a good idea in his mental state to attack him like she did. His heart maybe weak, not wanting her father to die with a broken one, but die knowing he was very much loved.

Closing her tired eyes into darkness. She peacefully focused her mind on soothing tranquil images like Gunnar McKay. Smiling while knowing he is the man she will live the rest of her life with, until she is too old and weak to live any longer. Resting in a spiritual world filled will miraculous angels, knowing her mother has been her guardian angel for years and soon to be with her father.

She looked towards the window, seeing the most beautiful sky she has ever seen. She said quietly, 'Mom, I know you are out there. I see a flickering star and I know this star is you. This cabin was your favorite place, as it is mine. You can rest now for I know where you are. I love you and will see you every night at his time. May peace be with you and soon with Dad. I love you Mom.'

She smiled in a sad way, but also in a loving way. Missing her deeply and learning to move forward. Closing her tired eyes into darkness, until morning rises above the mystical forest.

Waking up fresh and so alive, Anna Maria felt revived and free, as if she were an angel herself. She loved the fresh scent of the early morning air and wet dew gliding over the many miles of open land. Breathing calmly and again taking in all the beauty of what God created for all of us to cherish. Moving slowly, capturing breathtaking views of miles of open land. Enjoying the quietness and peace, she enjoyed all of what surrounds her, from the wild to the open blue skies.

Believing in time Gunnar and her would experience once again the beauty which surrounds her. Praying it will be soon and she so deeply wishes her father will deny his dying wish.

Two days had passed, Anna Maria embraced every waking moment. She spent hours exploring, viewing open lands and peacefully smiling in the inside. Enjoying the beauty of it all and never looking back. Not wanting to go back to the city, except witnessing Gunnar behind glass windows.

In her mind, all she could think about was Gunnar. Not a minute went by when a vision of him didn't appear in her head.

She suddenly turned sad. Thinking why is love so difficult. Why must she hide her feelings and desire for one man she loves more every day? Still wondering though why he deserted her and now reappears. She believes something bad did happen, praying he did not do anything evil or illegal. Time will tell. Hopefully everything dissipates, leaving her once again happy and very much in love.

A gentle breeze triggered among the open air, sending chills down her spine. She turned away from the fresh waters, looking upwards and facing his precious face.

She gasped, Gunnar you are here. How did you know where I was?

He smiled, reaching for her tender body. He spoke, I have not seen you in a while. Where else would you be. Your favorite resting place and of course our secret hideaway.

She just smiled, 'Gunnar I love you. What took you so long?

Deeply and romantically they kissed. Holding, breathing and listening to each other's heartbeat. Each heartbeat pulsed smoothly and rhythmically.

Anna Maria glanced down towards Gunnar's chest, moving rapidly, piercing through his pectoral muscles.

Leaving her motionless and craving for his irresistible body.

No words were spoken. No need to speak, for they could clearly read each other's mind.

A peaceful setting one they both truly loved. No need to express any emotions for this is what they both call paradise, quiet, hidden and far away.

Whenever Gunnar and Anna Maria travel miles and reach this secluded area their bodies become paralyzed and mind eases into a comatose state leaving them both incredibly safe and sound. Loving what they have cherished together for many years and praying their dream place never comes to an end.

Embracing deeply, tenderly and romantically, Gunnar smiled openly. He stood proud strong and gently kissed Anna Maria's chilled lips. He faced his beautifully lady raising her chin with his gentle touch. He spoke, 'Anna Maria, I have always loved you. You are the most beautiful and intriguing woman I have ever known. When I'm not near you I feel, as if you are inches away. Every minute of the day, visions of your contagious smile continuously play in my mind. You make me crazy. We will never part again, for I need you more today than yesterday. I love you Anna Maria.'

He bent forward kissing her tender cheek and reached into his coat pocket. Opening her petite hand and placing a fragile box in the center of her palm.

Her eyes suddenly filled with dampness leaving her limp, nervous and excited like a little girl.

He whispered, 'Anna Maria will you marry me?'

She cried, 'Oh Gunnar I love you. Yes, I will marry you. I was beginning to believe this day would never appear. I am the luckiest and happiest woman alive.'

Her patience had retired. She was dying to see what was inside of the jewelry box. She slowly opened it amazed and stunned at what she saw. Two carat square emerald ring with diamonds on each side.

She whispered with fresh tears in her eyes, 'You remembered.'

He smirked, 'Every time we would walk down Michigan Avenue you would go out of your way to glance at this ring. I knew this one was for you.'

She spoke sincerely, 'Gunnar I do not know what I would do without you. You are my knight in shining armor and you just rescued me.

He spoke gently and curiously, 'What did I rescue you from my love?'

She paused for the longest time. Rehearsing in her mind what comforting words to say. She spoke from all the pain in my life.

He smiled, 'You are free. I will protect and love you for the rest of our life. You make me feel so incredibly happy. Anna Maria, this is our home. I cannot wait for the day when we have precious children and share with them what we have grown to love. For now, let us enjoy these quiet days. Make passionate love for hours and rewind back to our future.

She rested her head on his chest and breathed in his unforgettable scent. Tearfully and softly she cried. Releasing no words, for she felt blessed to have beautiful memories and Gunnar McKay always near her side.

He reached for her hand leading the way towards the dense woods. Walking side by side just smiling for their love has always meant to be.

Hours passed. The mood of the forest seemed to change, swaying Anna Maria and Gunnar towards another direction. Back to safety, comfort and their special hideaway. Learning the mysterious sounds of the woods and wild, for the nightfall was near. Jogging a little quicker they laughed feeling a little alarmed. Fear of being in the center of the forest near dark, for the call of the wild roam out of their territory and explore for adventure.

Reaching the end of the path they both inhaled deeply. Trying to catch their breath, as they slowly walked towards the patio. Once again hand in hand admiring the beauty of the lake.

Fresh tears streamed down her face.

Gunnar spoke, 'What is wrong?'

She inhaled deeply, 'Gunnar, I do not want this day to end. I have missed you so much.' She cried tenderly never wanting to let go of him.

Holding strong not to cry Gunnar replied, 'Anna Maria, I'm so sorry for what I have put you through. We will be man and wife. Never departing again, for I love you more than words can say. No one will ever take you away from me again. Not power or money. I need you and love you very much. Do not ever forget it. '

He could see a curious look in her prominent eyes. Not wanting to ruin the mood and sexual embracement he reached for her. Leading the way towards the bedroom loft, inching his way towards her tender lips he smiled. She felt dizzy, excited and weak. Looking into his eyes feeling vulnerable, she quivered.

He pierced her with his hypnotic, eyes slowly placing her on the bed.

She could barely move, loving the passion and excitement they have for each other.

One by one each piece of clothing slid to the floor. Removing her satin panties last, while teasing her with his magical touch.

She did the same, first tossing his shirt to the side, then his jeans gently and sneakily touching his hardness, while pulling down his boxers. In a provocative way she gently licked nearly a second on his outer core, sending him in a state of urgency. She teased him enough and loved watching him melt.

He repositioned his body and arched up. He gently kissed her small, round and moist lips. Moving his mouth towards the bottom of her ear, clearly knowing what does excite her in bed. Licking her hard nipples and placing his hand between her inner thighs. He loved to arouse her, as he touched and licked each pleasure point on her petite body.

She wanted this evening to last to eternity, but they both knew they could not hold on much longer.

He lunged forward using his strength in his upper arms to hold himself upright. Slowly moving inside of her teasing and pulling out. Reaching for her breast and gently gliding his hands across her nipples. Arching downwards facing her most pleasurable area and finding he sensitive erotic spot.

On impulse she arched up and down. Spreading, moaning and inhaling each breath of air.

Wanting him again inside of her, Anna Maria reached for his muscular shoulders.

No resistance.

She whispered, 'Gunnar.'

Teasing for a few more seconds he responded. Inch by inch he licked his way to her tiny lips while feeling her body melt for his deep penetration.

He buried his inner thigh strength inside of her exhaling and inhaling with each rhythmically movement. Sinking deeper as her secretions motioned, leaving her wet and delicious.

Not a scund in the air except two heartbeats pounding as one.

Sealed lips, closed eyes and heightened muscles flexed his skin. His bare body tensed with each robotic movement. He was near knowing she was minutes away. Desperately trying to hold strong with slow and gentle penetration against her sweet and tender area.

Worn and tired he whispered, 'Are you near.'

She gasped.

Moaning, shivering and exploding at the same time. Sharing a climax so explosive and powerful. They both collapsed into each other's damp arms.

She felt as if her sensual organs would never end, as if multiple orgasms continued to pulse between her inner thighs. She quivered, arched and forced out a heavy sigh.

Rolling to the side staring her tired eyes he smiled. Whispering, 'I love you.'

In return she did the same. No movement still feeling totally aroused, worn out and delightfully pleased.

She giggled, 'I cannot stop flinching. My whole body is numb. I have never had this feeling before. Let's do it again.'

He rolled over facing her he laughed.

She smiled while closing her eyes.

He just stared at his lady, loving her more and more. He thought in his mind of how beautiful, faithful and above all how genuine she really is. Watching her sleep deeply he realized how precious life really is. Rehearsing in his mind how to explain their breakup. Not wanting to hurt her or her family. He knows it will not be easy and she may never want to see him again, after he tells the truth. Wanting to run away and hide, for fear of losing Anna Maria again, even if it shall endanger their relationship. No power or money will ever get in his way again. He will fight like hell and this time he will win.

Closing his eye into darkness he smiled. Gently holding his beloved lady and peacefully fading into a deep and sound sleep.

Hours had passed. The sun was slowly rising. It was 5.00 am, never too late for him to start a new day. He had always been an early riser. Loving the peacefulness before his hectic workday begins. Except today is not a busy day. It is a beautiful day of solitude and sharing his peaceful day with his beautiful woman.

She slowly walked down the stairs. She looked more beautiful today than yesterday. A natural beauty with soft olive skin, dark eyes and long black hair flowing from her cheeks down to the middle of her slender spine. Wearing her sassy glasses, his button tailored shirt and his overly large moccasin slippers made especially for him. Her face freshly rinsed, eyes tired, but a woman who looked as, beautiful as the night before. She smiled, good morning.

He could not take his eyes off her. He thought in his mind how ravishing she is and who will age gracefully.

He watched her though the double doors, reading the paper, sipping warm coffee, as he prepared her favorite breakfast, fresh fruit, scrambled eggs and wholewheat toast. Trying to keep still he wanted so badly to stay, but he knew time was scarce. He had only one more day with her before heading south. All night in his sleep rehearsing in his mind when and where to tell Anna Maria about her father. Right now, all he wanted to do is just deplete that part of the conversation from his mind and wanting to enjoy the remaining hours with her.

Carrying out two beautifully decorative planters he placed on in front of her. He smiled 'Enjoy'.

No words were spoken, as they both quietly ate. Eyeing one another after each bite and then turning towards the calm waters.

Minutes went by. She finally spoke, 'When are you leaving?' She already looked sad and lonely before he had even left.

He said, 'Later, at nightfall.'

She eyed him, 'Do you really have to go?'

'Anna Maria, I would love to stay here for days,' he said. 'I will be back if you are planning on staying.'

She looked so sad. He could see her eyes fill up with fresh tears.

They both had so much on their minds, but not sure how to release their messages.

With no hesitation he asked, 'Do you love him?'

She replied, 'What?'

'Come on, Anna Maria, you know, Antonio.'

She softly cried, 'No, I do not love him. I have never loved him. I cannot stand it when he is near.'

He asked curiously, 'How did you to meet?'

She paused for the longest time, 'My father.'

He swallowed hard, feeling his heart pulse heavy, growing angry in the inside. He was having a difficult time trying to control his tension and hatred for her father.

He said, 'Explain.'

'Explain what?'' she said. Why are you treating me like his? Remember you are the one who left me. I did not go looking for love. I patiently waited for you to come back and now I get treated like I committed a crime.'

He spoke underneath his breath, 'Did you sleep with him?'

She began to cry even harder, 'Why does this all matter? No, I did not sleep with Antonio. There, are you happy? Is that what you wanted to hear?'

'What about your engagement. Antonio said you were engaged.'

She sobbed, 'I never said yes. I do not love him, never have. I love you. Why are you asking me these questions? Remember last night. I said I will marry you. I'm engaged to you. I have been waiting for that evening for a very long time now. I love you Gunnar.'

He drew close reaching for her, as she collapsed into his muscular arms.

She spoke, 'Gunnar, I have missed you so much. I love you more than words can say.'

She sobbed, 'I need to confess to you. I have been holding a secret from you.'

'Go on,' he said.

She inhaled deeply. 'My father hired Antonio. He has no faith in me and wants Antonio to be president of Cecola & Gold when he dies. His dying wish is for me to marry Antonio and no one else.

'That is why I'm here for the first time in my life I came face to face with my father. Telling him all, from how I do not love Antonio. He makes me ill whenever he is near.

'I told him he would destroy Cecola & Gold. My father believes women should rest at home and have no careers. I cried and screamed my true feeling at him. He did not even open his eyes. I know he heard it all. I told him I'm in love and not with Antonio. I'm praying he wakes up and we peacefully can talk again, for he does not have much more time. I strongly vocalized I do not wish to honor his dying wish, for I would be resting peacefully within a year with my mother above the great gates of Heaven. I would die with a cold and broken heart, because of his ego. One man who gets whatever he wants, except this time.'

She paused, 'I walked away saying long as I'm alive, Antonio would have no part of Cecola & Gold. I'm in love, Daddy, and there is nothing you can do. I strolled away without turning back. A few moments later returning and apologizing, before I traveled here up north.'

His mind was racing with disturbing facts so much information triggered in his head. Desperately trying to be calm, not believing what he had just heard, but he did believe all. He knew all along her father was the biggest snake in Chicago.

He sat for the longest time comprehending it all.

She did not move or say a word just fresh tears streaming down her chilled cheeks

She finally spoke, 'I never want to leave our secret hideaway. Life is so simple and peaceful here. Why must my father be so difficult?',

His lips remained sealed biting his tongue wanting to come face to face with her father. Giving him his piece of mind and saying he is weak and a coward. Money buys whatever he wants. Well he is destroying his one and only daughter.

He spoke sincerely, 'Anna Maria, I'm so sorry. I had no idea.' Holding her tight, embracing her pain and breathing in her beauty. Feeling horrible for making her sad, angry and relieved she loves him and not Antonio. He clearly understands now of all that has happened in the last year. Knowing what needs to be done, for now cherishing the remaining hours with his beloved future bride.

They returned indoors, as she followed each one of his steps. Trailing behind slithering her shirt to the floor. She watched him intensively, as he removed his sweatshirt, boxers and sweatpants. Tossing them wherever they had landed. He reached for her hand, sliding the shower door to the side entering playfully.

She smiled patiently waiting for his passion and fireworks to begin.

Slowly turning the shower head to full stream, he turned facing her engulfing all her energy. First, he kissed her slender neck, to her inner ear, back to her tender lips. Hugging underneath her fragile arms with his tensed arms and gently rising her up. Moving beneath her and slowing entering. Holding strong as his muscles pulsed with each deep penetration.

She moaned enjoying the steam bath as it pulsed hard against her body. She truly loved the sensational feeling as

Gunnar slowly moved inside of her. He could feel her moist female secretion creating more pleasure and enjoyment. Stroking her vagina and touching her most pleasurable spot. Feeling her body warm, weak and spicy hot. Breathing heavy air thin and thick she was near he could tell. He teased entering, departing and seconds later nipping at her erect nipples sending her weak organs into unstoppable convulsions. Her body was melting with much anxiety. Wanting to release and explode giving more time for the ultimate extraordinary feeling.

He whispered now, 'Anna Maria.'

Giving into his command she let go. Arching upward with her eyes sealed she whispered, 'Yes.' Moaning with full pleasure feeling his wetness penetrate inside of her.

He continued moving inside of her thrashing her thighs and feeling her tiny body pierce against his. He stopped strong fast with great explosion.

She was short of air. He was still inside of her. Her body fluttered feeling another sensation. A wonderful feeling a multiple climax.

He did it again a man who knew his woman well. Giving the ultimate excitement and pleasing her to the point of weakness.

He moved slowly outward smiling and feeling remarkable. He said, 'I love you.'

She stood weak closing her eyes and facing the pulsing waters still quivering and smiling. She whispered, 'I love you, Gunnar McKay.' Opening her mouth and have rushing waters flow down her tired body.

He grabbed her from behind. Holding strong for support for his body was weak and very much fatigued. Resting his face on her upper back he inhaled.

Listening to her heartbeat as it slowly pulsed back to normal. Pulling away and leaving her alone. Smiling as he reached for his towel. Feeling like a man as he once again pleased his lady as she did the same. Together they shared intimacy, tender touches and the greatest gift of all, love and happiness.

For the rest of the day they talked, walked and held hands as if they were on their first date. Taking in all the beauty of the dense forest and watching the calm waters edge against the shady shores. Breathing in the crisp air and feeling special to have such an extraordinary lake house.

Gunnar spoke softly, 'Follow me.'

They rustled their way through the deep path hand in hand. Stopping inches away from the Cecola family paddle boat. 'Well, come on,' he said.

She smiled, remembering in her mind the quiet evening they had. Escaping in the night and venturing out with the stars, moon and few boat lights flickering in the dark night. They secretly vanished as the gently waves pushed them out into the middle. Sharing a bottle of wine and staring for hours up in the open and dark skies. Witnessing a falling star never a word for they both made the same wish. Smiling and glancing at one another naming the formations of the stars which seem so close to them and very much brilliant. Spending hours close together and sharing a special bond only a few have experienced.

She whispered, 'Gunnar, it is so beautiful out here. I believe it is just as beautiful now as it is ever.'

Nature was all around them from the wild edging the outer woods. The birds flying among the open skies, to the creatures breathing underneath them.

Ever since Anna Maria was a little girl, she has always appreciated the great outdoors respecting nature and their habitat. Learning the calls of the wild and what animals roam near. Researching how they live and sharing her knowledge with Gunnar.

'Look Gunnar she said pointing up to the sky. 'There she is.'

He smiled, 'she still is around.'

'Of course, she will live for a very long time. I think she remembers us. Isn't she the most beautiful creature you have ever seen?'

Gunnar could not keep his eyes off Anna Maria. She carried on talking highly about the great eagle. Saying at one time they were almost extinct and now their habitat has risen.

She smiled, 'Gunnar you may think I'm crazy, but I think this eagle follows me because of my mother. You know I believe her spirit lingers over this open lake. Her childhood was this lake and I believe the great eagle sends messages of how she is still near. Shortly after she had passed. My father, cousins, uncles and many friends spent nearly a month here. From the moment I stepped outside.

I saw her perching on an old willow tree, only a few feet away, eyeing me in a peculiar way. Sailing above me and then landing near my foot. I bent down, afraid yet feeling comfort.' Starving for words she said facing Gunnar, 'I saw tears in her eyes. A wild eagle staring at me not moving and dripping with tears. Do you think this is my wild imagination, because I miss her so much or is my mother out there? At night I see where my mom rests high above the open skies, flickering and shining. She is the most beautiful star enhancing the open skies.'

Sitting quietly Gunnar smiled. Not releasing any sound from his sealed lips for the longest time. He knew Anna Maria was not crazy just a grown woman with a broken and lost heart. Missing her mother deeply and believing she existed spiritually.

Reaching for her hand he spoke tenderly. 'Anything is possible. If that is what you want to believe, then believe. I do know this eagle seems to come from nowhere. I wonder where she lives.'

Anna Maria smiled, 'Over there beyond the horizon, pointing to the open skies.'

As they paddled back to shore peace and tranquility filled the air. Not a sound or word. They both knew the day was coming to a peaceful end. Once the boat was anchored, he could no longer hold the emotions in.

Reaching for her. He felt her pain. He whispered, 'This is not the end. We will be together soon. Everything will be all right. I promise. Soon we will be man and wife, spending each waking day together.'

She softly cried, 'I love you.'

He passionately kissed her, holding her he whispered, 'You know, I must leave and go back to the city?' Trying to get words out he was already gone.

She walked back to the cottage like a little lost puppy. Crying softly, as he drove away, saying you never told me why.

Chapter 7

Standing inches from Mr. Cecola, Gunnar glared. Minutes went by. He patiently waited. Wondering when he was going to open his cowardly eyes. Rehearsing in his mind what words to say. He glanced over to the monitor. Thinking maybe he was near the end, but he was very much alive. Breathing, inhaling and twitching his fingers. Still staring he finally raised his head and slowly opening his eyes. Focusing hard and not believing what his eyes just came glued to. He quickly blinked them back to darkness.

Gunnar spoke harshly, 'You do remember me. You are weak and old. I can easily pull the plug. Give you misery, as you did me. Open your eyes.'

He cautiously lay still, not resisting. Slowly raising his eyelids and glancing into Gunnar's fearful eyes. Desperately trying to speak, he inhaled deeply. 'No, please do not pull the plug.' Stuttering, 'What do you what from me?'

Gunnar fired back. 'Do not play games with me. You know damn well what I want. The only person you care about in the world is yourself. You can care less about

Anna Maria and you know what. I truly believe she will never see you again.'

Gunnar knew how to get his heart racing and that was to talk about his one and only daughter. Making him believe she wanted nothing to do with him. He smirked, 'How long has it been since you last saw her?'

His eyes turned cold, body flinched, and face turned beet red.

Gunnar laughed. 'So how does it feel to be on the other side. Dying alone and feeling much pain.' Reaching in his pocket he pulled out a check for one million dollars. He shoved it near his face, toying with him and shredding it into tiny pieces. 'You thought you got rid of me. Well, I'm here to stay. Your money and power no longer matter. I love your daughter and you will never come between us again., not even all the money in the world. You really think you just pay people off. I came to my senses. You should see your daughter. She once again is very happy. I destroyed her trust, because of you. What makes me such a bad person. I know it is because I do not kiss your ass like everyone else. I'm not afraid of you. Remember you are so weak and soon to be out of mine and Anna Maria's lives. Why must you be bribing and making choices for others. Is it because you like being in control or merely power? The only power you have is money. Anna Maria does not care about what you leave her. All she wants is to be happy and me by her side. Cecola & Gold means so much to her. She realizes how hard you have worked and does not want anyone to destroy what you have created.

You have no faith in her daughter. You treat her as if she still is a little girl. She is a grown woman. Respect her and let her move on.'

The room was silent for the longest time. Gunnar knew his mind was racing. He deeply wanted to know what thoughts traced in his head.

Shaking, Mr. Cecola spoke, 'Where is my daughter?'

Gunnar paused, 'She never wants to see you again. You destroyed her mind, for nearly a year. Persuading her to marry a man she does not even love. What do you get out of it? Believing you had just won again. Well let me tell you something. You have lost for the very first time and you will die with a broken heart, because you lost Anna Maria many months ago. She is not going to marry Antonio. She will become my wife and I will treat her like a princess just like you have. You can believe what you want, but Antonio is just out for your money. His ego will interfere with your business and in months Cecola & Gold will diminish in time.'

He lay still, as peaceful as the night. Eyes sealed, throat dry and his dying heart beating for his beautiful daughter. In his mind, he dreamed of her. Praying she comes back to him, for he needs her more now than ever.

Antonio is weak. He was an easy victim. Gunnar used his charm just like him and smoothed his way into Cecola & Gold. For weeks researching and studying the architectural field. Meeting him at a convention center and later socially having a couple of beers. Antonio grew fond of Gunnar and hired him on the spot. Never telling Mr.

Cecola or anyone else, for he knows how to play the game. Hire the intelligent, play all day and in return earn mega dollars to put in his burning pocket. His whole life he had to charm his way to get what he wants. Not having much of a childhood and stealing his way to the top.

Gunnar had learned a tremendous amount about Antonio, his lies and cheating on innocent victims. He is a con artist and smoothed his way into Cecola & Gold. Gunnar will not rest, until the family knows the truth. His whole plan was just to reach out and take his woman away. Finding out more than he ever wanted. Now he must free Anna Maria from her pain and delete Antonio from the picture. Sending him back where he came from, nowhere.

Gunnar said in a persistent way, 'Don't you have anything to say? I'm good for your daughter. You know money means nothing to me. I never cashed your check. You tried to pay me off. What do you think Anna Maria thinks? You robbed someone she truly loves, because you do not care how she feels. Love and happiness are everything, not power or money.

'I want to see Anna Maria,' he said in a painful way.

'What makes you so sure she wants to see you,' Gunnar replied, 'I'm sure she has no kind words to say to you. '

'Please,' he said, 'I'm begging you.'

Gunnar hesitated, 'Why? So you convince her to marry Antonio?'

Mr. Cecola pleaded fighting back tears. He could no longer speak, for he was so exhausted and weak.

Gunnar watched him as his breathing became still, eyes closed and his mind sealed into darkness. Pondering in his mind what he was dreaming. Dreaming for forgiveness, for his dirty actions or fighting like hell for his dying wish. Gunnar himself prays he does not find out he works for Cecola & Gold. A slip of the tongue could ruin everything for him and Anna Maria. Keeping quiet and sticking to his plan. Praying this whole mess comes to an end before it is too late. Knowing Anna Maria's father is slowly dying and in a short time will remain silent.

In a few days he will be back with Anna Maria. Telling all for he prays she will forgive him and her father's bribery. Convincing her to talk to her father and convince him to get rid of Antonio before it is too late.

Gunnar smirked walking through the corridor, feeling like he had defeated the bull. Turning back, standing, facing and curiously thinking what games play in his head. Eyes wide, wet tears and lonely emotions traveling down his pale and worn face. He was beginning to feel sorry for him, painfully dying and all alone. Watching him intensively he suddenly felt cold, ashamed and bitter. Trying desperately to forget about the past and move into the future. Forgetting about the bad and learn to forgive. Forgive a man for what he has done, for he deeply loves his daughter and only wants the best for her.

Gunnar eyed him curiously, knowing from his dreadful expressions, he does have feelings inside of his cold body. Wanting to reach out and give him strength and courage. Saying everything will be all right and his daughter will always be in good hands.

He smiled facing Mr. Cecola behind a pane glass window. Thinking in his mind, one day he will be his son-in-law feeling as if he had already passed. Wanting only acceptance from him, closing this chapter and beginning a new one.

Chapter 8

She stood a few feet away looking beautiful and vulnerable. What changed her mind. Why did she come back so soon? Smiling, missing her beautiful eyes and precious features.

Gunnar spoke, 'I love you Anna Maria.'

She read his lips. Bowing her head forward trying to hold back her laughter. She was so glad to see him feeling rather warm and dizzy. Arriving back to the city early, just to see his precious face and being near his side. Arching forward gracefully smiling and melting for his desirable body.

He winked tenderly and so passionately.

Miles too far she no longer wants to be alone. All she dreams of is Gunnar day and night. Never giving up hope and prays her father will honor her wishes.

Inhaling deeply, breathing in his masculine scent. Loving everything about him. The stylish clothes he wears. The way he combs his hair and how his piercing blue eyes send her mind and body into a ritual trance. She smiled feeling her heart flutter. She closed her eyes thinking about him. His tender ways and magical touch. Oh, how she loves Gunnar McKay.

Entering through the double doors leading to the elevator she inhaled deeply stepping forward and taking a ride for her life to the lowest level. Watching each green button disappear counting the floor numbers until the elevator came to a complete stop. She slowly exited feeling calm and relaxed. She nearly lost her breath. There he was standing proud, arms folded resting along a stair rail. Smiling looking so handsome and positive.

He smirked, 'Well, what took you so long. I was hoping you read my mind.'

She laughed, 'What are you talking about?'

He just stood there staring.

She said, 'Well what is on your mind Gunnar McKay.'

He paused, moments later speaking calmly as he stared into her beautiful brown eyes. He whispered, 'We do have a lot to talk about. I was hoping you would follow me. There is a little Italian restaurant off the beaten path. Secluded very well kept and quiet. Meet me there in one hour. You will love it. It is called Bubba's.'

He watched her intensively as she exited the building. She was everything a man truly expected from a grown woman. Beautiful, courageous and a smile that is so contagious.

He did feel nervous and quivered thinking how he was going to explain why he made such a quick departure. Wanting to tell her everything, for fear of her departing and never speaking to him again. Knowing deep down this was not going to be easy. Pondering tender thoughts in his mind, as he drove, entering in the restaurant, praying she will listen and believe.

She was already seated, waiting patiently, snuggled in a dim corner. The flickering candles amplified her extraordinary features. She was ravishing, stunning and so sensual.

He spoke, 'Anna Maria you are so beautiful.' Smiling and bending forward, gently kissing her tender lips. He whispered, 'I have always loved you.'

Her heart fluttered, eyes teary, mouth moist. She felt so alive and very much loved. Never depleting her feelings towards him and always feeling the same way, as if each date was the first one they have ever had. Enjoying each other, as if there will never be a tomorrow, feeling her heartbeat pulse rapidly every time he is near. Wondering in her mind if her sensual feelings towards him will ever slowly fade away and the sparks in her eyes remain explosive whenever he is in sight.

There is never a good time or calming words to say, but he knew in his mind now was the best time to tell her the truth.

He stared into the distance for the longest time. Rehearsing in his mind what to say. He paused, 'Anna Maria I really do not know where to begin.'

She swallowed hard thinking the worst. She said, 'Go on.'

He smiled, 'I never stopped loving you. You truly need to believe me. I never wanted to leave you. I had no choice.'

She asked curiously, What do you mean you had no choice?'

He hesitated, 'Please just listen. You know your father never was fond of me.'

'Yes,' she said. Bracing herself and feeling teary welled up eyes.

'The early afternoon on the evening I secretly vanished from your life. Your father and his bodyguards followed and trailed me until I reached the harbor. I had no idea why they were circling me, as if they had a message to send. They did have a message. A very painful one.' He inhaled deeply, 'This is very hard for me, Anna Maria.'

She insisted, 'Continue.'

His face said it all, pain, flushed and sadness. He whispered, 'I was scared and very weak. Your father expressed strongly. He never ever wanted to see me again. To leave and never come back and if I did. I would never walk again. He handed me a one million dollars check. If I did not accept, he would have me sent away. He just laughed do not mess with me boy. Get the hell away from here. You better be gone by tomorrow morning or else.'

Tears streamed down her chilled cheeks. She did not know who to believe. She cried, 'I thought money does not matter to you. You were bribed and left me for one million dollars. How could you?'

Before he even had the chance to say. He did not cash the check. She was gone. Furious, hurt and so disappointed. He did not know what else to say, for he was so wrong to take off. Mr. Cecola certainly was the culprit of his own game, causing pain to his one and only beautiful daughter.

He sat for the longest time. Thinking of her. Praying she would come to her senses and if not, he must somehow deal with the painful situation. Living life once again without the woman he truly loves.

She cried in the parking lot, for what seemed like hours, until no more tears would shed. Turning painful and emotional tears into rage. No more sadness expressed on her face, just fire. She was trying to focus hard and comprehend everything Gunnar had said to her. Thinking in her mind, is her father truly the villain. How could he. He has always been the most caring and sensitive person she has known. Is there really a dark side to him? Why has she never seen him act dirty or evil. Is the Cecola's family reputation to be shamed or to be proud of? She has been in the dark since she was a young child. Protected supervised and never alone. Is there a secret. Should she find out the truth or honor her father's wish and marry Antonio. Maybe he is right. This is the man for her. She cried how could you Gunnar. Feeling alone, desperate and eager to learn the entire truth. Knowing one thing, she does love him. Why must everything always be so difficult? Who will she choose?

Chapter 9

Standing inches away she inhaled deeply. Watching him intensively and wondering what thoughts were in his head. He has always been so strong and courageous. Now he lies still, calm and suffering into a slow and painful death. His eyes each day look weaker and weaker, for soon his lids will no longer open. They will remain sealed and he will spiritually travel to another world full of angels and with his beautiful wife once again near his side.

Each minute is crucial, finding the truth before he is too weak to speak.

She whispered, 'Daddy are you awake.'

His eyebrows arched up, eyes wide and a gigantic smile appeared on his pale face.

He spoke, 'Anna Maria where have you been. I missed seeing your beautiful face and tender smile.'

She paused for the longest time. She said, 'I have been around.'

A puzzled look expressed in his dying eyes and aging features. He sensed more trouble from her. Wondering if Gunnar had told her what he had done. Is Gunnar to stay and with Anna Maria?

She whispered, 'How have you been. I see the nurses and doctors are taking good care cf you. It is a beautiful day. The bright sun is shining in your direction. It is your day today.'

He had no idea what she meant by that statement. He was not up for her games. Wondering if she was going to get right to it or play with his head.

He finally spoke, 'What is it Anna Maria? What do you want to tell me?'

She stood still, arms folded pondering deep thoughts in her mind. She hesitated but spoke in an honest way. 'Daddy, why would you hurt me like that. I thought you were an honest and trusting man. You have broken my trust in you. I truly love Gunnar. I do not know who to believe. I should believe you because you are my father. I should believe Gunnar because I want to marry him. You paid him off. I was crushed and for nearly a year. I thought he left because of me. Why would you do such an awful thing and tc own flesh of blood?'

He was trying to speak, but no words were forming. Minutes later he no longer felt weak and his strength triggered to his highest level in weeks. He spoke brokenly, 'He is no good for you.'

She fired back, 'What on earth are you talking about?'

He blinked, 'Only Antonio.'

'What makes him so special. Every man I ever dated was never good enough for you. Why do you think I hid my relationship with Gunnar and the end you found out?

You destroyed me. I will never forget. He is the only man I ever loved. You and Gunnar no longer exist in my heart.'

Pacing his room Anna Maria felt so bitter and hurt merely by her father.

He lay still, clammy and cold as a stormy winter night.

She spoke, 'You are not even sorry are you?'

No response.

'I want to know something. Did Gunnar leave because of your power, money or did you threaten him. For years now you have had bodyguards trailing your feet. You must have done something dirty, illegal, deadly or Daddy, is it just you acting the part? Showing off what you have. Having others believe you need protection and for what reason.'

He was fighting back tears, eyes strained, muscles tensed and still no response

With no hesitation she said, 'I do not love Antonio and never will. Only if you knew the truth. You can care less. You only want to believe what you clearly think he is about. He certainly has you fooled. No one has ever charmed their way into your arms like him. Think about it. Just because he is our kind or maybe he is not. I know you have always said Italians marry Italians nothing else. Well honestly, I believe he is merely acing. Tell me something Italian about him. He has you so convinced. You are so wrong about him.'

Silence filled the room for the longest time.

After several minutes she finally spoke. 'Gunnar is everything I ever wanted in a man. Just because he is Irish does not mean he is not a good man. He is beautiful, courageous and a human being who does not deserve to be with our family. You cheated me out of love and paid him off. I can clearly see why he took your money and left me behind. Why would he want to be around a man like you? How could he survive marrying into a family and having a dreadful father-in-law like you? Who is crooked and dishonest?

He lay motionless. Closing his tired eyes. In his mind wondering why she does not know the truth. He saw Gunnar tear his bribe check into tiny pieces. She believes he took the money and ran. What happened? Why does she still believe he cashed a one million dollars check, written by him.

She saw a puzzled expression appear on his stone cold face. Wondering what disturbing thoughts were in his mind.

'What are you thinking,' she whispered? 'Why must you always get your way. If Mom were alive, she would be furious.'

He fired back, 'She isn't.' Wet tears dribbled down the side of his tear ducts.

She eyed him intensively. I know you have a warm heart. Just please let me go, love and live my own life. I will be miserable for the rest of my life if you make me marry Antonio. If that is truly what you want, then I shall honor your wish. She walked away without even saying goodbye.

Chapter 10

Hours turned into days. Days turned into weeks. Each waking hour Anna Maria became more tired, nauseated and very much alone, except for Rosie her housekeeper of many years. She checked in on her regularly behind closed doors.

Very much wanting to be in her father's shoes, wanting to close her eyes and never reopen them again. Only to see her beautiful guardian angel. Her darling mother, Mary Catherine.

Every night for the last few weeks, she had the same continuous dream. First her father saying marry Antonio. He will be a good husband. Moments later waking out of a deep sleep and reentering into another vivid dream. Gunnar whispering Anna Maria I love you. I'm so sorry.

She desperately was losing her mind. Not wanting to ever leave her childhood castle room, until she makes her final decision. She had no other choice, but to marry Antonio.

Rosie was stunned as Anna Maria slowly moved towards her. She had not seen her in days, hidden all alone. She was so thin, pale and unfinished. Rosie drew her arms out. She whispered what have you done to herself. Moments later, she collapsed on the tile floor.

Rosie gasped, 'No Anna Maria wake up. Please my child, do not go. Holding her tightly against her chest. She whispered, What has he done to you. Please beautiful girl wake up.'

Gazing into Rosie's teary eyes, she said, 'Who?'

Rosie used her strength and helped Anna Maria off the cold floor. They both entered in the living room, aiming directly towards the overly sized sofa. All her strength and muscles were deteriorating. She was so fragile and anemic looking. Her beautiful olive skin no longer looked vibrant, with a pearly soft finish. No facial expressions just looked badly battered and neglected.

Placing a damp cloth on her head. She spoke quietly, 'Anna Maria you need to get strong. What on God's earth is happening to you.? Is it your father?'

Tears streamed down both women's cheeks.

Rosie was always there for Anna Maria. Taking her in when her mother passed at a very young age. They grew fond of each other. Held personal secrets in and taught one another to be strong and courageous.

Rosie knew all about Gunnar, from his mischievous ways, entering the mansion and leaving early in the waking hours. They came face to face. She smiled and gave him a precious wink.

He whispered thank you for not saying a word. He kissed the side of her check and secretly dashed past security. She truly admired his spunk and knew deep down he was the man for Anna Maria. She thought any person brave enough to enter onto the Cecola's grounds was a strong and persistent individual. She did like Gunnar and till this day does not know what had happened to their hidden relationship.

Rosie spoke softly, 'Anna Maria speak to me. I'm here for you. Please tell me all.'

'Please Rosie not now I'm so tired.'

She vocalized strongly, 'That is all you have been doing. You need no more sleep. Get up and get your life back into order. You need to be strong for your father. He is the one dying not you.'

Anna Maria stared motionlessly into Rosie's eyes. She whispered, 'My heart no longer feels pain. I'm cold I died weeks ago.'

Rosie shouted, 'Look at yourself. You are a beautiful woman, but now you look as if you have been sleeping in a dumpster for months. You have never acted like this in your entire life. What on earth is wrong with you. Is life really that bad. If you should feel sorry for anyone it is your father not you.' She walked away angry, livid and breathless.

Anna Maria was beyond tired but was shocked at Rosie's words. She has never treated her this way ever. She cried saying to herself. Now I have no one in my life.

Rosie heard every word and came storming through the double doors. She said, 'Do not feel sorry for yourself. You know I have always been here for you. How can I help you when you cannot help yourself? Whenever you are ready to talk. I will be here and waiting patiently?'

Rosie marched back to the kitchen banging on pots and pans. Wondering in her mind what drew Anna Maria to go into a great depression. Thinking in her mind. Gunnar merely has been gone for a year. Her father is slowing dying and Antonio seeks and loves her. What made her beautiful mind depart from society. She was going to get to the bottom of this even if it shall endanger her life with the Cecola family.

A few days went by. Rosie had noticed Anna Maria was touring the house more. Showering, applying makeup and walking the terrace. Each day was a struggle, but Anna Maria fought like a Cecola and grew strong, felt fresh and wiser than ever.

One evening, she slowly entered the sunroom where Rosie was reading her favorite novel, *Wings* by Danielle Steele.

She casually asked Rosie, 'Have you ever been in love?'

She was taken back by the statement but was so happy Anna Maria was merely back to her normal self.

She smiled, 'Yes.'

No words were spoken for the longest time. Anna Maria stared out into the daylight and Rosie eyed her novel. Curiously wondering, why she had asked her the question?

'Who was he?'

'What?' Rosie said.

'You know, who you were in love with. What was he like?'

Rosie placed the book on her lap and folded her glasses. She smiled, 'Robert. He was nine years older than me. I was nineteen.'

Anna Maria hesitated, 'Well go on.'

Rosie smiled, 'He worked for my father's landscaping business. I fell in love with him right away. I would watch him from the corner of my eye whenever he was near. We both sensed each other's emotions right away. I knew he was the man I wanted to marry.'

Suddenly the room became chilled, saddened and still as if a phenomenal presence had just entered the glass room.

Anna Maria sensed Rosie was having a difficult time expressing her words. She said, 'I understand. You do not have to continue. I'm sorry I even brought it up.'

Rosie smiled, 'Please stay, Anna Maria. I have not spoken about him in years. Robert was a good man. I deeply loved him even how young I was.' She looked at Anna Maria smiling. 'We hid our relationship for the longest time. It was almost two years before we said anything.'

Anna Maria smiled. She knew exactly how she felt. Wanting to know more without any hesitation she asked opening. 'What happened?'

Rosie grew tense. She became fidgety and her voice crackled. She spoke painfully. 'My father was angry. He became belligerent, alarming and violent when I told him about me and Robert. No, he screamed. My daughter does not belong with an older American. You are too young. I forbid you to ever see him again.'

Anna Maria swallowed hard. She said I am so sorry.

Minutes went by. All her facial expressions disappeared. She looked worn out and sad. Releasing a hidden memory for so long and sharing it with someone she deeply admired. Smiling, feeling teary as she closed her eyes and visualized Robert in her hurt mind. She whispered, 'I never saw Robert again.' Choking for words. She said, 'All I have are beautiful memories. I deeply wish I could see his face just one more time.' She then bowed her head into the palm of her hands.

Anna Maria was fighting back tears feeling the pain Rosie had experienced many years ago. She said, 'Rosie I do not get it. He just took off and left.'

'Yes,' she said. Looking at Anna Maria she half smiled. 'He did love me. We even talked about getting married. I believe my father was the culprit. Robert never worked for my father again. He somehow and somewhere just disappeared. I prayed everyday he would return, but he never did. I still do not understand why all of this had happened to me.'

Anna Maria reached for her hand saying, 'I'm so sorry.' She embraced Rosie in her arms and they held each other for the longest time.

Rosie spoke silently, 'When I realized Robert was not coming back. I packed my bags and left home. I never talked to my father again. Years ago, I attended his funeral knowing that was the right thing to do. My mother died when I was young. I had no siblings. My father spoke very little English. I learned quite steadily throughout my years in America.' She smiled as wet tears penetrated her saddened eyes. She said, 'If it was not for your family. I do not know where I would be today. Your father saved me and my sanity. You are my family and I love you all very much. She was choking for words. I do not know what is going to happen when your father passes. She began to cry.

'Oh, Rosie do not cry,' Anna Maria said. 'You are not going anywhere. You just said this is your home as it is mine. No one is leaving.'

Rosie smiled, 'I do not know how to repay you.'

'Repay me?' she said. You have done enough. You have kept this family so alive with your laughter. This is the Cecola home and you will be here forever.'

Rosie softly cried into the palm of her hands saying, 'Anna Maria, thank you will all my heart.'

They sat still admiring the beauty Rosie had created for them to all share. A beautiful rose garden filled with extraordinary beauty only a few have ever seen.

Rosie eventually spoke Anna Maria, 'It is your turn to confess. I have never told my deep inner secret to anyone only you. Now I want you to tell me all from the beginning to the end. What makes you melt in your room for days. Never leaving or speaking of your pain.'

Anna Maria hesitated she inhaled deeply. 'Where do I begin?'

'Just take your time,' Rosie insisted.

Anna Maria began speaking brokenly, cracking her words and mumbling. Not quite making any sense.

Rosie reached for her hands. She simply stated, 'Please slow down and relax.'

She took a deep breath speaking about Gunnar McKay. She told Rosie how he had disappeared for nearly a year and how they fallen in love all over again. Explaining how he had proposed marriage and gave her a beautiful emerald ring.

Rosie threw her arms around Anna Maria crying, 'My baby girl is engaged. I'm so delighted for you. Does your father know?'

'No,' she said, Daddy must not know.'

'Why Anna Maria why?'

Breathing heavily, she broke down desperately crying. 'Gunnar left me because of Daddy.'

'What?' Rosie said curiously.

'He paid Gunnar off. Gunnar and I met for lunch and he told me everything, from all of Daddy's threats to the one million dollars he gave him to disappear. Never to see or talk to me again.'

'Oh my God. My dear child. This is horrible.'

'Gunnar is working for Cecola & Gold. Antonio hired him and Daddy does not even know. His dying wish is for me to marry Antonio, or I will not inherit Cecola & Gold. I receive nothing. I do not love him.'

Rosie smiled, 'You love Gunnar.'

She bowed her head. 'I thought I did.'

'What are you talking about Anna Maria? Are you crazy or sick in the head? '

She cried, 'I cannot believe Gunnar took Daddy's money and ran.'

Rosie spoke brilliantly, 'He came back didn't he?'

Anna Maria mumbled, 'Yes and with one million dollars in his pocket.'

Rosie looked straight into her hurtful eyes. She whispered, 'What makes you so sure he took the money. Why would he return to the windy city, if he had spent the money? It just does not make any sense. He came back for you and only you. Not the money or Cecola & Gold. I saw the way his eyes sparked every time he cleverly escaped through the patrolled grounds. Waiting for you to wave before he exited.'

'How to you know all of this?'

Rosie smirked, 'I have my ways. He is a good man. He loves you and do not ever deny your feeling towards him. I was wondering what had happened to you two. Now, I know and believe me do not terminate this relationship or you will be very sorry and extremely lonely. You need to speak to you father.'

'I have,' Rosie. 'I have. He thinks Antonio is gold and the man I shall marry. I am beginning to believe Daddy is right.'

Rosie shouted, 'You just stop right now. He is wrong. You fight for your man. Talk to Gunnar again. Maybe there is something missing in this story and maybe he did not tell you something important. Please I'm begging you

Anna Maria. Please listen to me.' She paused, 'I lost the only man I have ever loved. I did not fight for him. I was afraid of my father and what he would do. Do you realize how bad I still hurt? Till this day I often wonder where he went or even if he is alive. I do not want you to ever feel the way I do. Living with guilt my whole life and losing a beautiful man for no reason.'

Anna Maria sobbed, 'My father will never change his mind. Do you know, Rosie, he never ever met Gunnar? I just do not understand why.'

Rosie gave a charming and healing smile. 'Your heart will make your decision for you. Remember being happy is everything.' She then kissed her cheek. Gave a precious wink and walked away teary eyed.

Anna Maria sat still for hours, thinking about her conversation with Rosie. Realizing they had so much more in common then she had ever imagined. Sharing intimate secrets, crying and holding one another for comfort. She felt terrible for Rosie. Losing the only man, she had ever loved, but feeling blessed having her near for many years now. She thought in her busy mind of how bizarre her story of losing Robert was so similar with hers. Yet, Robert never came back into her arms, but Gunnar did. Remembering how difficult it was for him to speak badly about her father. Knowing Gunnar is a good person and what will she do next, only time will tell.

Chapter 11

Weeks had gone by. He was beginning to lose his mind. Why had she not returned his calls or shown her beautiful face behind the glass window in his view. The haunting images of her hurtful face has depleted from his stone, cold mind. She was beyond hurt. He could clearly tell and understand why. He was beginning to believe she had disappeared just like he had. Frantically in his mind thinking of the absolute worst. Wondering though how could she leave her dying father all alone? From the beginning he was the cause of their inner pain. He knew Anna Maria was too kind and warming to avoid her father in his mental state and mind.

Antonio has come and gone. Showing his pitiful face and leaving without a trace. Gunnar wondered in his mind if he had spoken to Anna Maria and her family lately.

Not saying much to him either, as if he were a nobody working underneath him. Just simply as an employee and nothing else. He often wondered what were his intentions. Does he really love Anna Maria? Soon he will find out, convince Mr. Cecola he is worthy and not Antonio. Praying Anna Maria in time will take his hand in marriage.

Closing the door behind him. He walked once again out the empty building alone, tired and exhausted. He searched the full lot. Eyeing his Mercedes Benz and exiting the garage gates closing behind him.

Minutes later driving slowly through a shady area. Seeing homeless people huddled together. Shading themselves from the drizzling rain underneath their old and ratty newspapers. Debris and garbage were scattered everywhere among the deserted streets. Bums were digging through garbage cans and some sat hopelessly with a tin can. Praying someone drops some money into it. It was not a pretty sight to see and even experience. Not a squad car or police officer in sight. He knew the only way to get to his destination was to travel though these depressing and violent streets. Leaving before dusk and quickly fleeing before trouble starts.

Curiously eyeing abandon buildings and praying his numbers did not match. He traveled two blocks forward feeling a little more at ease. Seeing less poverty and more of his kind. A hidden voyage, only a few have heard about.

Turning towards a somewhat vacant rehab building and parking inches from the main door. He sensed curious eyes inspecting his every move. Feeling like he was being watched and monitored from every direction. He kept sight of his Mercedes, as he pushed the call button and waited for a reply. Clearly looking over the tattered building, which was bolted down with black rod iron fences. Again, he pressed the button waiting patiently. He was just about to leave when a stern, tall, dark skinned man came walking down the stairs.

He strongly vocalized, he said, 'What do you want?'

Gunnar swallowed hard, 'My name is Gunnar McKay. Teddy Johnson referred me to you. He said you could help me.'

He spoke, 'Come on in.'

Gunnar watched him from the corner of his eye. He acted nervous, paranoid, looking over his shoulder before locking the steel door behind him.

The narrow hall leading to his office smelled musky and moldy. It was hard for him to catch his breath from the pungent order.

A tattered sign hung from the door.

It read

Private Investigator

Charles Webb

STEP IN AT YOUR OWN RISK

Gunnar inhaled deeply not quite making out the quote he had just read on his door. Thinking to himself. What kind of character is this man?

So, he said, 'You know Teddy Johnson.'

Gunnar hesitated, 'He is my cousin.'

'No shit,' he said.

'Welcome make yourself at home and what can I do for you?'

Gunnar reluctantly spoke, 'I was wondering if you can help me.'

'I'm listening.'

'I need some information on a certain individual. I believe he is not who he says he is. Do you think you can help me?'

'First all this may take some time.'

Gunnar spoke instantly, 'I really do not have much time. That is why, I'm here.'

Charles eyed Gunnar intensively. He asked, 'Are you in trouble?'

'No, no I'm not. I just need to have this information be for it is too late.'

'Before it is too late. What do you mean by that statement? You must be in some kind trouble or what else is it. I cannot help you if you do not give me as much information as possible. I need a lead, names for reasons why?'

Gunnar was uncomfortable and Charles could easily sense it.

'Look Gunnar he said. I know you must be a good guy if you know my buddy Teddy Johnson and to refer me to you. This is big. He must have great trust in you.'

Gunnar inhaled deeply, 'There is this guy.'

Charles smirked, 'A woman is involved right? I should have known.'

'No, no,' Gunnar said. 'It is not what you think. She is not a two timing girl. This guy works for her father's company and he is seeking to take over the corporation.'

Charles asked curiously, 'What is the company name?'

Gunnar looked him straight into his curious eyes. He said, 'Cecola & Gold.'

'Oh man, you do not mess around. How did you get involved in such a family as the Cecola's? Better watch your move as you speak. Did you see if you were being followed?'

Gunnar swallowed hard, 'Yes.'

'This gets even better and good. Go on,' he insisted.

'I dated Michael Cecola's daughter for quite some time. We hid our relationship and eventually we were caught. He offered me one million dollars to hit the road and never see his daughter again. Michael Cecola and his men surrounded me at the pier with guns in their hands. They were not messing around. I left for fear of my life and never told his daughter Anna Maria why. For nearly one year I had vanished and eventually came to my senses and that is to get my girl back no matter the circumstances.'

Charles lit a cigar eyeing Gunnar wearily. He said, 'Go ahead tell me all. '

'When I arrived back to Chicago. I had no idea what I was going to do, until I was having a drink at a local pub with Teddy Johnson, my dear cousin. We overheard Antonio speak of how he is going to take over Cecola & Gold. For days I trailed his every move. Wondering how he charmed his way into the Cecola family. I followed him to a convention center and that is how we met. We had a couple of beers and now I work for Cecola & Gold.'

Charles inhaled deeply blowing out a gulf of smoke. He spoke, 'What! Are you crazy, and did you represent yourself. Does father Cecola know?'

Gunnar smirked, 'It was rather easy. I just played his game. Charming my way as he did his. No Michael Cecola does not know, but Anna Maria does. Antonio Maggiano is up to something. '

'Wait a minute,' Charles said, 'Did you say Antonio Maggiano?'

'Yes, you heard me.'

Charles paused, 'He is one bad apple.'

'What do you mean,' Gunnar said?

'He has been around.'

Gunnar spoke, 'If I do not find out the truth about him soon. Cecola & Gold will no longer be a powerful corporation.'

'Mr. Cecola's dying wish is for his daughter to marry Antonio. She will inherit all, but Antonio will have the power as president. I recently spoke to Anna Maria and told her all. Since that day I have not seen her. A few weeks ago, I asked her to marry me, but now I feel she will honor her father's wishes and to marry Antonio.'

'What happened to the one million dollars?'

'I shredded the check into tiny pieces over Michael Cecola's chest, as he lay sick in his hospital bed.'

'You did what?' Charles said. 'You are one brave person. You must really love this woman, or you are totally crazy.'

'I'm not crazy,' Gunnar said. 'I want to find out the truth, before it is too late. I believe Anna Maria will marry Antonio just to please her father, even if she does love me. She is very angry that I had left.'

Charles hesitated, 'Does she know you never cashed the check?'

'Before I could even tell her, she was gone.'

'Well that makes a difference. You need to find her and tell her the truth.'

Gunnar spoke, 'Can you help me?'

'Of course, I can help you. This will not be cheap.'

'Whatever it costs.'

'First let me tell you. You always need to watch your back. Make sure no one is following you and please be careful. I will get back to you in a couple of days. This is not a family to mess with. They are very powerful. Since Antonio has become close with Michael Cecola be wise. I will lead you the way.'

Chapter 12

He could not hold on much longer, acting the part. Trying to be someone he is not. Sooner or later his scheme will all come to an end. Tumbling down hard on him if he does not make a quick move.

There she was walking proud, beautiful, vibrant and full of life. She smiled.

He nearly lost his breath. Stumbling, catching his cell phone, as it rang Give Me Shelter by the Rolling Stones.

He glanced down not comprehending the unfamiliar number. He answered, this better be good.

Eyeing Anna Maria, as she strolled by his window. Wanting to reach out to her, but instead heard a deep voice say, 'Hey, Gunnar, it is Charles Webb.'

Damn it, Gunnar said silently. Absolutely bad timing, but desperately wanting to hear what he had to say.

Charles spoke, 'Are you alone?'

'Yes,' he whispered.

'Good, now listen closely. This character Antonio has a bad track record. It all started as a child. Living in the Bronx. Cheating and stealing his way to the top. Dropping out of high school and traveling around. Living in major cities and staying, until he had gotten what he eventually came for. '

'I'm listening,' Gunnar said.

When he was eighteen. He was sent to prison for robbery, out two years later and back in again. He mainly preys on women who are extremely wealthy. It does not matter the age or looks. Leaving them alone, empty and depleted from any spending. This is a continuous cycle for this man.'

Gunnar interrupted, 'Can you get me paperwork on him?'

Charles chuckled, 'Who is the detective here, you or me? Of course, I have everything you need. Meet me at my office as soon as possible.'

Before Gunnar could even thank Charles, no voice, the tone of his cell phone was silent as the night.

He smiled believing he may have won Antonio's game. He keeps on playing. Searching every direction. So deeply wanted to grab Anna Maria into his arms. Should he seek for her now and try to make peace or venture out. Walking towards her office. Getting a glimpse of her beautiful tender body he smiled. Turning in the opposite direction. Straight to the elevator doors. Moving quickly and swaying his head to the right.

She looked puzzled but gave a brilliant smile in return.

His mind was busy. Wondering if he had made the right decision. Leaving her empty and alone once again. Knowing though Charles Webb's message was extremely important. He eagerly wanted to find out the disguise

Antonio has played throughout his life. Wanting him clearly away from the Cecola family and miles away from Chicago's city limits.

He raced through every street, never looking back. By passing every red light, until he came within blocks of Charles Webb's barricaded building.

He nervously looked over his shoulder. Eyeing every hoodlum, bums and a few gang members slowly driving by, looking suspicious and up to no good.

Gunnar swallowed hard wondering why Charles' practice was in such a remote area. Polluted and disgusting. Was he really an investigator or someone who portrays to be who he is not? At this point, he really did not care who Charles was. In his mind, he knew he had the right man to do the job.

Before he was out of the car Charles had greeted him.

They shook hands and proceeded to march up the narrow and scummy stairs before entering though his office doors.

'Well,' Charles said. 'You will be quite interested in seeing the paperwork on this guy. He has a rap sheet extended to the floor.'

Gunnar asked curiously, 'Is Antonio this deranged. Why does not Michael Cecola not know about him?'

Charles chuckled, 'He is a con artist. This is what they do for a living. He smoothed his way into the Cecola family like he did every other corporation, women and families. He is brilliantly smart and lucky, but not anymore.

Gunnar smiled, 'The papers are all I need.' He handed Charles a sealed envelope, saying, 'Thank you.' Turning the doorknob and just before exiting he heard a raspy voice speak.

'Gunnar this is way more than I had requested.'

'Keep it, you deserve it. I may need you in the future.' He exited, without even turning back.

Jumping in his car. Unraveling Antonio's rap sheet and feeling a rush of anxiety. Driving away, glancing down towards his hands to get a glimpse of Antonio's unruly life between every stop light. Cruising like a maniac to reach his destination. A tiny local pub, blocks away from Cecola & Gold headquarters.

Resting in a corner hidden from all, he unrolled the overly large piece of paper. Concentration on the first few sentences. He read

Antonio Maggiano last alias named used.

Birth named Chester Brown born in 1961,
    father William mother Emily.

First arrest age 10

Second arrest age 12

Third arrest age 15

Dropped out of high school and ran away from home. Never did he return to his birthplace. Never saw his father again.

Parents are now deceased. No known siblings or relatives.

Used many alias names and changing his identity after every victim.

Gunnar knew Antonio was a snake, but never realized how crooked, evil and wicked he really was. One continuous game that he has played for many years now. This time has walked his way into danger and not even realizing it. His glory days are over, for he will rot behind steel bars and this time will never be released.

He smiled, thinking in his mind the hard part has just begun. Knowing it was going to be difficult in convincing Anna Maria to speak to him but knew he must fight like Hell.

His mind was racing. Wondering if he should be the one to tell Michael Cecola about the man he truly admires, or his only daughter to speak of words he so deeply does not want to hear.

Will he believe or shut his eyes back into darkness.

The truth will be told. What more does he need to hear or see?

Regardless Antonio will be caught. Not in Cecola & Golds corridors, but elsewhere.

Still smiling he inhaled deeply. Visualizing in his mind what expressions lies on Antonio's face when he is confronted by a mob of police officers. No way out, but back to the cell.

He could not hold this information in about Antonio much longer. He was like a small child trying desperately to keep a sealed secret. Wanting to reach out to Anna Maria and tell her everything. Promising her that life will be sweet and simple once again. He knew though her hot

Italian temper would get in the way. He smiled knowing exactly what he was going to do.

Chapter 13

Again, Antonio was not in sight. No car smell of his smutty cologne, or presence. He clearly never is in close distance or in places he said he has been in. One continuous cycle soon to be no more of him and his pitiful lies, disguises and fraudulent ways.

A tapping on the window startled Anna Maria. She slowly raised the blind and sent it right back down.

Without any hesitation he turned the doorknob before she had any time to even think. He was near her side smiling. Staring at her with his intense serious and deep blue eyes.

She said, 'What brings you here?'

He replied, 'You are coming with me.'

'Like hell I am.' She glared fearlessly

He smiled, 'Well, you do not have any choice.'

She asked curiously, 'What do you mean?'

'If you do not come with me. I just may kidnap you.'

'Are you crazy?' she said.

'Yes, I'm crazy in love with you.'

'I'm not leaving.'

'Oh, hell you are.' He then proceeded to grab her hands. Wrapping them around her mid back and placing his left hand over her mouth.

She tried to fight and scream, but he was so incredibly strong. Thinking in his mind what possessed him to act this way and take her away. Where was she going. Was he crazy or just madly in love with her?

He spoke, 'Listen to me, Anna Maria. I have something very important to show you.

'You must go with me. Do you understand?'

Her eyes were wide open.

He felt horrible for scaring her like this, but he knew this was the only way to get her attention.

He whispered in her ear now, 'Anna Maria. I'm not going to let go of your hands. Do not even try to run.'

She swallowed hard. Feeling almost frightened, as her heart and veins bumped with rushing blood.

'Now, Anna Maria, be calm and stay near my side.'

The front desk attendant did not even look up, as they calmly walked through the front doors.

He opened the car door helping her inside and immediately locking the Mercedes doors. He entered cautiously, staring at her intensively.

She was furious. 'You did not have to be so rough. What has gotten into you?'

He fired back. 'What has gotten into me? What about you Miss Princess.'

She was hot. 'Do not ever call me that name again.'

'Well now I finally have your attention. If you weren't so bullheaded like your father maybe I would not have to kidnap you.'

She snapped, 'Do not bring my father into this.'

Gunnar glared over towards her. 'Remember your father is the one who started this game and I shall end it.'

'What do you mean?'

'You soon will find out. Try to relax and get comfortable, because we have a very long drive.'

Anna Maria's mind was racing with disturbing and some sensual thoughts. Wondering how he could be so cold, ruthless yet so charming, passionate and kind. What was he up to and what kind of game was he playing? Soon she will find out praying it is all good and not bad.

He smiled, knowing he disliked the sad expression lying on her face. Never having an encounter like this with the woman he truly loves. Their first major fight since they have been together. He giggled still sealing his lips. What was next, feuding over wedding arrangements? Deciding on a big or small reception. Who will be the best man, maid of honor and where to rest on their very important day?

He suddenly turned sad thinking maybe she really has changed her mind. Not wanting to marry him because of her father's dying wish. Praying Michael Cecola will be strong.

No words were spoken for the longest time.

Gunnar sensed coldness, darkness and disturbance from the corner of his eye. She sat alone and worn out expressing curiosity in her tired eyes.

He no longer could keep his lips sealed. He said, 'Anna Maria please do not be mad.'

She smiled, 'I know you would never hurt me only in my heart.'

He was speechless. At one time he ripped her cold heart leaving without a trace. Now he sees sadness once again on her pale face. Hating how he has betrayed her and kept a deep secret hidden from her for many months.

'Gunnar', she said, 'why are you acting so bizarre and mad? You are like a different person. Sneaking behind me, grabbing my arms and kidnapping me. You know it is a crime.'

He placed his hand gently on her thigh. He smiled, 'You did not resist.'

'I had no choice.'

'Sure, you did.'

She finally smiled, 'All I ever wanted was to be happy.'

'Well, are you?'

She hesitated, 'You make me so alive.'

'You did not answer my question'

'Yes.' She then closed her eyes.

He watched her doze off and on twitching her arms, as she fell into a light sleep.

Moaning, 'Oh, Gunnar, I love you.'

He smiled eyeing her tender, beautiful and petite body. Wanting to lift and carry her into a bed of roses. He loved her more at that moment then he had ever. A ravishing beauty, one he has greatly grown to love and admire.

Gliding his fingers along the side of her cheekbone. He gentle slid downwards as if a gentle feather were brushing against her soft skin. He swirled his hand down towards her chin and back around her sleepy eyes. Feeling her lavish facial features. Admiring her shimmering complexion, as her beautiful skin shined brighter than the early morning sky. He was in love. A wonderful inner feeling one he has always kept close to his heart. Driving as if he were in a deep sleep himself. Rehearsing in his weary mind how to begin his conversation about Antonio?

She lay back against the car seat with her head arched sideways towards him.

He could watch her all day long with her beautiful striking black hair, curvy cheekbones, eyes so mysterious and mystical. Gently tweaking her overflowing bangs away from her face. He massaged softly up and down. He had always loved the elegance of long hair especially. Her dramatic eyes are one of the greatest features. They say something about a woman, for she has the power to hypnotize him with her piercing, dark, oval and paralyzing eyes. Complete strangers would kindly express that she had the most beautiful eyes. Wondering in their minds and asking without holding back asking if her lashes were real. She would always remark thank you. Feeling blushed a little embarrassed and expressing compassion. She is a strong woman. At times bubbly with a contagious laugh and a smile that never ended. Teeth white as the first fallen snow. Lips small and softly covered with a hint of shimmer pink gloss.

He smiled feeling alive with his lady by his side. Knowing at that moment they will have a life filled with great blessings.

Chapter 14

Gliding his hand down her face he patrolled her as if she were a statue on display. Looping his head forward whispering in her ear, 'Anna Maria we are here. Wake up my love and see paradise.'

She smiled not even raising her tired eyelids.

He said 'You are free now. You can run if you like.'

She smirked, 'Can I have a hint where you have taken and deserted me.'

'When I said I was going to kidnap you? It did not mean I was going to travel around the world.'

'Well, are you happy where I bought you?'

She said, 'Of course, the cottage. Thank you Gunnar I do truly love you. Please forgive the way I have been acting. I feel like I'm crazy. If it is not my father. It is Antonio or you and recently it has been Rosie.'

'What about Rosie?' he asked curiously.

I will tell you all about it later. Let's just enjoy a few hours holding, loving and being alone before we mend words. I really do not want to ruin the mood and spirit which surrounds us.

He knew to listen. Feel what she feels and concentrate on their togetherness sharing and romantically embracing.

She was the first to enter. Opening each window one by one. Feeling the crisp air and smell of fresh pine. Inhaling deeply, as the gentle breeze tickled her face. She smiled as he held her from behind. She spoke, 'I just love this view.'

He leaned against her. Kissing her slender neck, down to her protruding spine, licking upward.

She felt the temperature rise through his pulsing veins. He was warm, sensual, hot and vulnerable.

He whispered kindly, 'I have missed you.'

His muscles penetrated deep, hard and full. Feeling his arousing body against her she moaned with exhilarating passion. Loving how he held her strong, tight and warm.

Caressing her inner back with his muscular and hard abs. She could feel his body enhance with hardness, stiffness. His heat was so steamy and contagiously captivating.

She turned steadily facing his manly face.

He smiled engulfing her round lavish tender lips. Romantically twirling his tongue and feeling her body crave for his inner desire.

Wrapping her arms around his shoulders and feeling his chest muscles press deeply against hers. She smiled feeling more aroused then she has ever been.

Gentle gliding his hands down her petite arms and moving slowly near her tiny waist. Then passionately he massaged her warm breast.

She no longer was cold, but hot, sweaty and driven.

He loved the sensation against his palms, as her cold nipples feverishly danced playfully into tiny, hard, erotic, pleasurable love toys.

They had this desire for one another that was unstoppable.

Closing her eyes, arching her head forward feeling aroused by his manly ways she smiled.

He loved watching her twitch, thrust and breathe deep into his arms. He had this way of making her surly, sexy and above all prepared to make passionate love, until their bodies become limp, weak and lifeless. What a joy he had teasing her until she could take no more.

Leaning forward she reached for his muscular biceps, slowly bringing her tense body close to his.

Kissing, licking, peeling off his pressed tailored shirt she turned towards his piercing, paralyzing eyes.

He smiled, 'You are amazing.'

No words came from her sealed lips.

He could clearly read her speedy mind.

Reaching for her slender neck he gently kissed below her ear.

She moaned with excitement.

He whispered, 'I love you.'

She said, 'Do not stop.'

Never denying her sexuality as a beautiful woman. He treated her like a royal princess. Gentle touching, kissing, stroking, as if a light feather were gliding against her smooth satiny skin. He moved slowly up and down near and high. Ending with his mouth on her round luscious lips. Pressing her petite breasts against his warm, firm and protuberant chest muscles.

He teased her until she could barely surrender.

She deeply wanted to continue the ravishing foreplay, but he already had her lying bare and beautifully naked on the living room floor. She rested on one of the many quilts placed throughout the house.

He arched between her legs peeling them away. He glided his body upward embracing her pulsing body.

She helped him roll his pants to his ankles tossing them across the room.

He taunted her, as he slid in and out, between her breast and back in again. He continuously teased her to a point of luxurious pleasure before lingering her to the ultimate height. The turning point to a voluptuous climax.

'Gunnar!'

No response!

Playfully he quickly charged forcefully.

She knew it was time from his moan to his hardness and his rapid rhythm vigorously penetrating deeply inside.

Concentrating, she smiled knowing she was so near.

He moaned, as if he were on fire, piercing deeper.

Within seconds, after his explosion she arched up releasing openly. Moaning as he glided against her hot spot forcefully with full turbulence.

He continued to move allowing her great satisfaction.

Holding strong he could feel her body twitch uncontrollably. Her final tremor released. Her inner body stopped moving immediately.

He laid gently on her perspiring frame, kissing her neck, ear and back on her dry lips.

He whispered, 'I'm sorry. I could not hold on any longer.'

She just smiled loving the way he so deeply cared about her, especially in bed.

They lay side by side, holding, calmly breathing and cherishing the time they have with each other.

She asked, 'What are you thinking?'

'Nothing.'

'Come on, you are thinking about something. What is on your mind?'

He said, 'My mind is on you. I'm so glad you will be my wife. One year has gone by and what a jerk I was. Life is short and I learned the hard way. You are the most important person in my life.'

She smiled rolling to his side. She whispered, 'I love you.'

Chapter 15

Eyeing her a few feet away she looked more beautiful than ever. With her long flowing hair swaying in the light, gentle breeze. Her dark brown eyes penetrated the sun's rays. They glittered, gleamed and sparkled. Sending him into a highly contagious trance. He could watch her all day. One woman with natural beauty full of spirit and life. In his mind he was rehearsing phrases. Repeating them silently over again, until he was well prepared to take a major step. Sitting down calmly with her and explaining everything he had learned about the man who has interfered with their precious lives. It was hard enough for him to talk about why he had deserted her and now he must be patient again and tell all. Praying she does believe, for he loves her more every day.

Blinking the dampness away from his eyes he suddenly grew emotional. Never has he ever felt so temperamental towards anyone or any situation before. He took a deep breath removing wetness from his lower lip. The newspaper was no longer dangling in front of her face it merely fell upon the patio table. She looked distressed, weary and stunned to see him standing inches from her with such discoloration on his face.

She asked Gunnar, 'Are you all right. You look so pale.'

'Yes, I'm fine.'

'Are you sure?'

His lips remained shut. Walking towards her he reached and placed his hand on hers. He said, 'Where would you like me to begin. Should we sit here, take a walk, sail whatever you want.

'Gunnar you are beginning to scare me, you choose.'

Reaching for her she passively clasped her hand around his palm. Following his footsteps, as he led his way through a narrow path. 'Do you know what I really want?'

'No,' she said in an unsure way.

'I want you father to respect and like me for who I am. I'm having a hard time dealing with this vengeance he has against me. I need for him to honor us to be man and wife. His presence or spirit will be hunting me till my death. I want to marry into a family who will accept me into their lives with love not hatred.'

She swallowed hard. 'Does this mean you do not want to marry me.

'Of course not, I love you.'

'Then what are you saying?'

'Everything I have already told you. I need your help as well.'

'I have tried.'

'Well we are going to try again once we get back to the city. You do call Rosie daily.'

'Yes.'

'Good.'

Silence seemed to be lingering in the air which seemed like hours.

Holding hands, they walked, admiring the beauty that surrounded them. They stopped a few feet from the edge of the trail coming upon a sandy hidden lake. Taking off his windbreaker he pointed to have her sit down.

She obeyed him.

She shuffled her toes underneath the sand, as he skipped tiny pebbles across the surface of the calm waters.

He always had this talent of skipping stones never ending his quest, until he skipped at least fifteen in a roll. Standing tall he grabbed a handful of flat stones and continued his childhood game.

She loved to watch him.

He finally spoke, 'Do you want to try?'

'No.'

'Come on, it is easy.'

He reached for her hand. She extended and stood inches from his side.

Wrapping his arm around her tiny waist he smiled. 'Hold on like this and arch your hand on an angle.'

Not even close enough to call it a skip. Again, she tried it was a lot harder than she had ever thought.

'No, like this,' he said.

They were smiling and skipping stones. Laughing every time her pebble drove straight into the water.

He said, 'I know it takes a lot of practice.'

She laughed.

Sitting down, her mind focused not on Gunnar anymore but, her father. She was speechless for the longest time.

He turned around sensing deep pain in her face. He said, 'Anna Maria what is wrong?'

Staring up at him, she felt teary eyed. She spoke brokenly, 'What is going to happen between us. I need to know. I love you Gunnar and I also deeply love my father.'

Tears streamed down her cheeks.

He bent down facing her and wiped fresh tears from her face. He spoke openly, 'You need to listen to me. Do not speak, until I finished what I have to say to you.'

Staring intently, as she bowed her head forward.

'Antonio is no good. I have learned some very disturbing information about him. It is all true.'

She was just about to say something.

'Sss,' he insisted listen.

She shook her head go on.

'I hired a private investigator and he is very knowledgeable in his field.'

Her head protruded. He knew well enough to sense fear and curiosity.

He continued and stressing how important his words were.

Inhaling deeply, he released words from his sealed lips. 'Antonio is a pathological liar. His whole life has been one big lie, starting from his early teens up till now.'

She swallowed hard wanting to hear all, but was fearful of Antonio.

He continued, 'Anna Maria, this is all the proof you need.' Momentarily he pulled out a raveled piece of paper from his windbreaker and placed it in the palm of her hands.

She hesitated at first and looked up into his deep blue eyes.

'Would you rather have me read it to you?'

She whispered, 'No.'

Standing up she dusted the sand from her clothes. Unraveling the tattered sheet of paper, as her eyes became glued to alias one, two, three and more. Her heart quickened, eyes welled with tears and her mind raced with very disturbing thoughts. She walked from one side of the hidden inlet to the other side without leaving sight of Antonio's secret life. She felt cheated, used and threatened. Wiping tears from her chilled cheek she whispered, 'Gunnar what are we going to do?'

'Antonio's game has ended. He will be arrested and sent to prison for a very long time.'

'What about my father?'

'What about him?' he said. 'He needs to know everything.'

'What if he does not believe.'

'We have all the proof we need and if not. I'm sure the chief of police will be talking to him.'

She felt chilled, scared and nervous. She wept, 'Did he ever kill anyone?'

I really do not know. I'm sure if he did all information would be printed. If not, we just do not know.'

'Gunnar I'm scared.'

'Scared of what he said?'

'Everything, don't you understand? My father has a criminal working for Cecola & Gold. We did not even know. What if my father is involved?'

He felt numb thinking about what she had just said.

Minutes later he spoke. 'Why would your father have anything to do with Antonio when he clearly knew what he was all about? Having a stranger come in and deplete his capital. Come on Anna Maria he is a lot smarter than you think.'

'I guess you are right. Antonio would probably never been seen or heard of again if he knew about his history.'

Her eyes wandered down the paper trying to comprehend what she was reading. Numerous aliases, times spent in prison, stealing, cheating, robbing and the list went on. She felt overwhelmed, paranoid and robbed. She was pissed. 'I knew there was a reason I did not like this son of a bitch and my father wants me to marry him. He is out of his mind. God damn it,' she shouted. 'Just when I thought my life was going a little smoother. You throw this at me.'

'I'm sorry Anna Maria,' he shouted. 'What in the hell do you want from me?'

She sobbed, 'I'm so sorry. I did not mean that. I'm truly sorry. I do not know what to say, think, or how to react to all of this. My father is dying, and I have a psychopath trying to prey his way into our family. I pray he holds on a little longer. I need for him to fight like hell to stay alive and find out the whole truth.'

He inhaled deeply, 'What if your father still does not accept?'

She vocalized strongly, 'He better and will. How can he not for one thing you have just saved Cecola & Gold? Antonio, most likely would disappear and never be heard of again. Deplete Cecola & Gold from all their earnings and leave the family with nothing just where he came from nothing at all.'

Extending his arms forward she walked straight into them and rested her head onto his muscular chest. Breathing calmly, she closed her eyes.

He kissed her head.

She smiled Gunnar, 'I love you.'

He felt this sudden fear, as if Antonio was near and followed them as they did him.

'What is wrong?'

Anna Maria, does Antonio know where you are?'

She responded, 'No.'

'Has he ever been here before or know about the cottage?'

'No why do you ask?'

He felt more relieved.

She glanced into his eyes. 'This is our hidden hideaway. Why would I tell him?'

He smiled, 'Thank you.'

'Thank you for what?'

He pulled her into his arms for being Anna Maria and no one else. 'You really do love me.'

'Of course, I do Gunnar. There is no man in the world I want to be with and on the beautiful plantation than you. I could never think about sharing our secret world with anyone else.'

They held hands for the longest time, listening to two heart beats flutter as one.

He spoke sincerely, 'I'm a little concerned about Antonio.'

'Why?'

'I just wonder if he has any idea about us. If at all if he is suspicious.'

She smiled, 'Antonio, all he thinks about is himself. I'm sure he has no clue.'

'How can you be so positive?'

'Rosie is the one who brought me back to my senses.'

'How?'

'She convinced me life was bittersweet and gave me my will, courage and love back to life. We talked for hours. She told me Antonio had tried many times to talk to me on the phone. Rosie resisted, saying I was not well and could not communicate with anyone. She had resented him from the first day she had met him. She hesitated, but–'

'But what?' he smirked.

'She absolutely adores you.'

He smiled thinking back. Remembering her curious face, as he darted passed the guards.

'Do you know Rosie has always known about us?'

He grinned, 'I believe so.'

She had expressed to me any man brave enough to sneak their way among the Cecola premises was a man to be trusted and one who truly loved a woman who was protected by many.

She looked into his remarkable colored eyes. She said. 'I would probably still be lying half awake and half alive if it was not for Rosie. She is a strong woman and loved a man very much. Her father destroyed their relationship. Her story was almost identical to ours. One difference is her fiancé never came back, but you did.'

He held her tight, fighting back tears developing in his eyes

She whispered, 'Gunnar, I love you. I understand the fear you felt. I never understood why you had left. I realized thou my father has the power to destroy just like Rosie's father.'

He spoke quietly, 'I'm still truly sorry for what I had put you through.'

'No more disappointing words. I know how you feel.' She then arched forward and kissed him passionately.

Walking hand in hand through the dense path dodging overgrown trees limbs she looked up at him. She said, 'Gunnar, I would like to be alone when I speak to my father. I want him to know how I feel and what Antonio is all about.,

He answered, 'I understand and when?'

'As soon as possible sometime tomorrow.'

He was speechless at first. 'Are you escaping?'

She giggled, 'Of course not. You kidnapped me remember.'

'Yes, I do remember. This means there is no running or hiding.'

She smiled, 'I will never hide from you again. I promise.'

He gave the sweetest wink.' I'm your watch keeper and you are my prize.'

She laughed turning her head and seeing silhouettes of the sun's rays creeping its way to the end of the path.

No words were spoken, for they could read each other's mind. Time was scarce, for tomorrow they would be on a long journey heading back to the city. One big city filled with lies, bribes and a father who knows his daughter well. Hopefully he will deny his dying wish and honor her incredibility.

Chapter 16

Entering through the hospital doors she became chilled, frightened and nauseous. Smelling a death-like scent, one she has always remembered and will never forget. An overwhelming odor and one she will never get used to. Remembering in her mind as a child she would visit her grandmother weekly at St Andrews nursing home, having her near her side. A dreaded visit, but one her grandmother very much loved. An overwhelming pungent odor, of toxic supplies and death like smell filtered throughout the open building. Fresh air diminished as soon as the front doors slowly closed and then the powerful fumes would enter through her nasal passageway causing tremendous pain. Immediately she would feel lightheaded, nauseous and tired as if she would pass out. A continuous cycle, one that is so vivid in her mind, as if it was yesterday.

Calmly she walked towards the doors. Rehearsing in her mind what soothing words to say. She inhaled deeply closing her eyes and entering slowly. After a few seconds she opened her eyes. Rosie was by his side. She smiled, 'Anna Maria.'

With no hesitation she stepped forward.

Rosie gave her a sweet kiss on the cheek.

She suddenly felt ill, nervous and very much threatened.

Rosie turned her head in the opposite direction using her body expression instead of her eyes. Her face was stone pale and lined with hatred. She reached out her hand and escorted her lovely Anna Maria to her father's side. She said, 'He has been waiting a long time for your arrival.'

She smiled

Rosie spoke softly in her ear, 'Do not pay attention to him. I will insist that he leaves. She then smiled held strong and seconds later released her petite body.

'Daddy, can you hear me?'

'Of course, he can hear you, my dear.'

'Excuse me,' she said, 'I'm talking to my father not you.'

Antonio just smiled. He strongly vocalized, 'I'm so glad you are well. You do know your father has been very disturbed by your absence and I think we all have. Don't you think, Rosie?' he said in an arrogant way.

Rosie fired back, 'Remember I have known her since she was a little girl. She is a fighter. You certainly do not give her credit she deserves. She is strong just remember that. No one messes with the Cecola family.'

A voice from the distance interfered, 'Now, now Rosie.'

She smiled, 'Mr. Cecola sorry if we had wakened you.'

He gasped for words inhaling in and out. 'Rosie you have always spoken your mind.'

She fluffed his pillows. Placed a warm blanket on his lower limbs and kissed his forehead. Turning in the opposite direction she grabbed Antonio by the arms. She said, 'We must leave and give Anna Maria her space.'

He said, 'I would really like to stay.'

She snapped, 'But you are not.' One minute she was speaking in English. The next minute Spanish words were sailing right out of her mouth. Her hands were flapping in the air and her blood pressure continue to elevate.

She has always been a hothead, especially when she knows she is right. Not many people Rosie dislikes, but he was beyond hatred.

When Anna Maria was a child. Rosie always spoke bilingual only by mistake though. Whenever she became very upset. She automatically switched her speech to Spanish. Especially when Anna Maria grew sassy and ungrateful. She clearly knew to stop with her demands, persistence behavior, spoil mess and bad attitude whenever Rosie spoke in her prime language. The fireworks would clearly erupt. Michael Cecola even knew when to turn the opposite direction.

Her high vocals filled much tension in the room even as weak as Michael was. He could clearly sense it.

In the car on the way back to the city Anna Maria spoke for nearly an hour to Rosie about Antonio. Telling all and not leaving one bit of information out.

Rosie spoke sincerely, 'Anna Maria I knew he was fake all along. There was just something about him that made no sense. I'm just glad he will be exposed and washed away.' She wants this man sent away, for Gunnar and Anna Maria to be happy as she was many years ago. With a man she still dreams about every night.

'Daddy you look well.'

Inhaling deep continuous breaths, he spoke, 'I'm well because you are here. Why must you be so stubborn.' Two remained in the room. Anna Maria and her dearest father.

He spoke jittery, 'I have missed you.'

She hesitated but went forward, 'Daddy ,I really need to speak to you.'

'Antonio already told me.'

She was outraged. 'Told you what?'

'The wedding is on of course.'

'What on earth are you talking about?'

'The wedding will be here. In this room where I will be a witness and best man.' He smiled, 'I knew he was the right man for you.'

She was furious. 'There is not going to be a wedding and, Daddy, there never was. If you only knew what kind of person Antonio really is. You would never honor him as my husband. He is liar and impersonator. He has you fooled, or are you just involved as he is in his continuous games.'

He mumbled, 'You must go.'

'Why because you do not what to hear the truth. Someday you may hear a tap on the door, and it will not be anyone you know. It will be the police.'

He gasped for air reaching for his call button. Within minutes three nurses and two doctors came barging though the doors.

'What is happening?' Anna Maria shouted. 'Where are you taking him?' She was stunned. She raced down the long corridors searching for her father. Reaching the end of the hall she was frantic to see her father. Two large men on each side of him forcefully pumping electric shocks onto his chest. His body violently sprung upward, as if he were a rag puppet being tossed into midair.

'What is happening to my father?' she cried?

A nurse grabbed her. 'You must go.'

She resisted.

Two student male nurses walked by and heard the violence in Anna Maria's voice. They both restrained her body movement and practically carried her down the hall. The last thing she saw was one nurse closing her father's curtain right in front of her eyes. The young men were persistent and were able to calm her nerves down. Clearly explaining why? She was not able to be with her father in such a dramatic time.

Again, she was alone fearing for her father's life. Not wanting him to die this way, but to never to awake from a deep and peaceful sleep. She sobbed in the palm of her hands. Whispering, 'Why must my life be so difficult,' she said quietly, 'Please Lord free my father from his inner pain. Let him live his life longer. I cannot lose him now. For anger hurts and I merely want to say my last goodbye with a smile on my face and not hurtful tears shedding from my eyes. Please I'm begging you.'

Chapter 17

Days she sat near his side. Never did he blink, smile or turn his head. She clearly knew he had heard every single word from the very first moment she had opened one of his favorite books. *Wings* by Danielle Steel, just like Rosie's favorite novel. She read daily to him, as if he were a child. Reading slowly so he would not miss a word and see why *Wings* is a favorite novel of all times. A powerful story of how one woman was so devoted to be the first female pilot to fly around the world.

At times she would choke up as she read. Loving the story more and more. Closing her eyes and pretending she were in the cockpit with Cassie O'Malley. She imagined Cassie and her flying though the mystical clouds. High in the sky towards a calming setting, so peaceful and magical. A place that is so quiet and far away. Wishing on a falling star and smiling. A beautiful well written story of how love, honesty and a strong will can make dreams come true.

She took long breaks wanting her father to comprehend what she had read. Wanting deeply for him to realize how powerful, devoted and how strong she really was.

She sat by his side daydreaming, as if she were Cassie. Stranded, lost and alone, as her plane vanished from all the living. Wondering in her mind what Cassie had left behind. Broken painful hearts or loving and apologizing words yet released from her heart. Did she say her final goodbye, or seal any regrets not openly spoken?

Tears streamed down her cheeks knowing this was only a story. A story that haunts her, for she prays her father opens his eyes so she can apologize. Whispering in his ear saying how much she dearly loves him. Death is sad, but she believes there should be no skeletons floating in the air. He must open his eyes, for she will tell all. He then will leave this world. She will have no regrets, haunting and hateful memories of her father.

She slightly smiled, kissing his forehead and brushing the side of his cheek with the palm of her hand. She deeply believes in her heart he will survive. Just enough for her to say she loves him. A father every daughter could honestly say is their role model and hero.

She sat for hours visualizing deepest memories of her dearest father. Eyeing him continually and admiring his strong will. Smiling as if she were young again and seeing the joy once again appear in his stable eyes. She truly loves him, despite the bad. Wondering if his mind is working, or visions of darkness lies below his sealed lids.

A few weeks ago, he held firm, fighting back a sudden and abrupt heart attack. Still fading as his cancer eats has soul away, but a strong heartbeat until he must surrender. Soon to take his last breath. One man who had it all, but now a lonely individual who soon must say his final goodbye and leave this precious earth for another one.

Reading the last chapter, she softly cried. A beautiful well written novel of love, honesty, family and dreams. A happy ending and one she deeply desires for her own family.

Gentle placing the hard copy book on her father's nightstand. She leaned over and gave him a tender kiss on the cheek. She whispered, 'Daddy I love you.'

Walking away she felt exhausted, overwhelmed and extremely tired. Sleep is what she needed, but how could she rest with so much on her mind. Days had gone by with no communication from the outer world besides the inner voices from the closed hospital doors. She wanted to be alone with her father. Not allowing anyone to enter and all had to honor her words.

Time is ending soon. He must open his eyes. Crying as she walked to her car. Looking up to the sky, peacefully smiling as she looked in the direction of where her mother rests. She smiled, blowing her mother a kiss, bowing her head, leaving calmly and knowing who she must see first.

He watched her. Being mesmerized by her beauty and poise as a woman. He was inches away. He reached out and eagerly, she embraced into his arms. They held one another for the longest time. Keeping their lips sealed, for they had so much to say, but no time to speak. Soon everyone will know they were meant to be. No more hiding lies and betraying others. True words will be exposed from their closed lips and one day they will be man and wife.

Gunnar finally spoke softly in her ear, 'Anna Maria, I have missed you so much.' Kissing her slender neck, ear lobes and engulfing her lips. Passionately romantically and playfully kissing each other, as if they have not seen each other in months. It was just days which seemed like a year.

She pulled away smiling. feeling lightheaded and dizzy. She whispered, 'Gunnar, why must our lives be so difficult. Can we just disappear to a remote and hidden island? Only you and me. It would be so precious.'

He smiled reaching for her tender touch. 'It does sound wonderful. You know it is not possible. I can tell you this. Our honeymoon is going to be so incredible, secretive and beyond our wildest dreams. No one will ever find us.'

She smiled, 'Gunnar I love you. I cannot wait. I wish my dreams of peace, quietness and togetherness is today not weeks, or months down the road. I want to run and hide'.

'Anna Maria you need to be strong. You made it this far. Please do not give up. I'm begging you we need more time.'

Tears streamed down her pale cheeks. 'I want Antonio out of our lives and for my father to deny his wish. Why must love for another have to be so difficult. Why cannot we just live our own lives.'

He hesitated, 'You know, Anna Maria how powerful, wealthy and well known your family is by the press. All your father wants is you to be happy. Life of luxury and show no embarrassment.'

She smiled, 'I'm happy with you. Happiness brings laughter and love, not money or living someone's else's dream.'

Holding her tight, pulling away he whispered, 'I promise you everything is going to be all right.'

'How can you be so sure?'

'I just know trust me on this. Do not deny your trust in me, for I will fight like hell to have you near my side for the rest of our lives. Anna Maria, remember I have always loved you and I will never stop.'

Reaching forward giving her the sweetest tender kiss. Pulling away reaching for her hand.

He spoke calmly, 'Come, Anna Maria, you need rest.' They drove until they reached where Gunnar was taking her. He led her though the arched doors and entered slowly into a small room. Walking towards the patio doors she smiled, feeling as if she were in front of her family garden. Smiling as if Rosie were near and cherishing the beauty she has created over the years. She could see why Gunnar had chosen to live here. Far away yet close to it all. A spectacular view surrounded by plants, flowers, cascading waterfalls and tropical fish streaming the waterways. A little tropical paradise merely for just two. A city lot hidden by blushed gardens with two overly large wicker chairs and a cocktail table off to the side.

She spoke, 'Gunnar this is so beautiful. I never knew.'

'You never knew what. That a man can respect and love nature like you.'

'No, Gunnar, I never have been here before. I'm very pleased.'

He smiled softly kissing her cheek and turning his body towards the kitchen.

Minutes later entering back into his garden with a freshly open bottle of wine. Two long stem chilled glasses and a gigantic smile lying on his face. He poured her first glass then his. Kissing her romantically saying 'You are so beautiful. I love you.' Reaching for a stale loaf of bread. He reached for inches from the bottle of wine. 'Here,' he said.

'What?' she said.

'Watch me, he then tore the bread into tiny pieces, squatting down near the edge of the pool. Tossing one piece at a time and seeing three fish fight to be the first to swallow the soggy sinking bread.

She was mesmerized smiling and loving being by his side. Missing his charm and the way he made her feel. Never doubting him for one second. Seeing in his eyes the glow, passion and beauty he brings to life. Bending down near him she smiled. 'Is it my turn?' First teasing the fish with a shadow of her index finger and then slowly stirring the fish into circles. One looked to be the outcast lost and all alone. She drew her attention to. Gently tossing the bread above and watching the other two devilish fish attack their way first. She felt terribly sorry for the loner, for he gave up and swam to the other end.

'Well some days he wins and most of all he loses.'

She smiled, 'Gunnar, this is extraordinary, all the beauty that surrounds us. I never knew you were so passionate for such creatures and nature. Every day I learn more about you. I know now why I have always loved you.'

He gently kissed her cheek and poured a fresh glass of wine.

They sat for the longest time before any words were spoken. Taking in all the beauty, cool gentle breeze, an evening so calm and peaceful.

She turned her head towards him. She grinned, 'Gunnar, let's elope.'

Coughing a sip of wine back into his glass swallowing hard he said what? 'You want to elope.'

'Yes, wouldn't it be wonderful. No more worries, just you and I saying our vows alone.'

'Now you are acting crazy.'

'No, I'm for real. I want to elope.''

Do you really think everything in our life will be better?'

She smiled, 'Marriage is what we both want, agreed.'

He bowed his head trying to comprehend her spontaneous words. Is she right, or trying to hide her inner pain? Maybe eloping would be the right thing to do, but what about Antonio. Her father would be outraged if he found out. His mind was racing as he stared into the distance. Wondering if this was the solution and maybe no one would ever find out.

She said ,' What are you thinking.'

'What you had just said.'

'So, what do you think?'

'I really do not know what to think. You clearly caught me off guard. I do know this. You may be right. We are grown adults and can clearly make our own decisions. My only concern is your father.'

'He will never find out.'

'What about Antonio.'

'When we arrive back from our weekend away. We will get the police involved. Send Antonio away and confront my father about his past and with the police standing inches behind our back.'

'You make this seem so simple.'

'You know we can do it. This all is a lot simpler than you think'.

He hesitated, 'Are you at all not concerned, scared, nervous or rushing into a quick and easy marriage. Do you want more time to think this all out? What if something bad happens to your father and you are not there.'

Tears streamed down her tender cheeks. She half smiled, 'I want Antonio out of our lives. I need to know he will not inherit our family company. I know my father's wish is only verbal. He wants to break me down and have me marry the man he believes is right and run Cecola & Gold.'

He eyed her. 'You are telling me there is not a written consent that Antonio will inherit your father's company.'

'No!'

'What makes you so sure.'

'Trust me. My father would never just throw his company away. Ever since I was a child. I have always been vice president of Cecola & Gold. In writing it specifically says I would move up to president once my father is deceased.'

Gunnar's expression was puzzling.

She said, 'Why do you look so alarmed?'

'I'm trying hard to understand all of this. Why are you so afraid of Antonio running the company?'

'He will destroy what my father has worked for his entire life. My father's dying wish is for me to marry Antonio for he wants him to run the company. Like all men should and for me to shy away. Stay home like he believes all women should.'

'You said before if you do not honor his wish of marrying Antonio you would lose the company. Your name is clearly on your father's deed.'

She paused, 'I'm just to afraid Antonio has convinced him to rewrite his will. What if he already has. Do you think Antonio wants to marry me so bad, because he knows we wed before he can take over Cecola & Gold? I clearly believe I will remain president unless Antonio and I marry. Antonio is rushing into marriage and my father is insisting I marry him. My father would never have made this decision, if it was not for Antonio. I finally figured it all out. It is all about Antonio and his devious ways. Gunnar, we need to marry as soon as possible, for me to inherit Cecola & Gold entirely. I need to be married. I may not have a chance to own my father's company. Antonio figured it out. He went into the company's secret, closed and confidential files. He read everything. He pried opened the files and found my father's will. He must know something and I believe the records say. I must be married to inherit Cecola & Gold, for my father wants my husband to run his company.'

'You are right, Anna Maria. We need to run away, say vows and destroy Antonio before it is too late. Sooner the better, before your father's strength weakens and he can no longer breathe on his own.

Chapter 18

Today is the most important day of Anna Maria's life. Her very special wedding day. Dreaming of this day since she was a little girl. A memorable day filled with family, friends, beautiful flowers and the sound of church bells ringing in the gentle breeze. But there was no family, nor friends, or music softly playing in the background. Not the wedding she has always dreamed of. As a little girl she visualized in her mind of what she would look like. Seeing her father extending his hand and giving her away. Her face had saddened, as she looked in the full length mirror. Dressed in a white tailored suit, high spike heels, a soft short veil resting on her fitted hat. She did look quite ravishing, but not what a bride should look like on her wedding day. She looked more like if she were marrying for the third time. Thinking in her mind what her mother's dress had looked like. Seeing pictures of her as a beautiful bride. Believing one day she would wear her mother's special gown. Wonder in her mind if her mother would ever forgive her or praise her for what she is doing.

Walking towards the window she clearly could see the small chapel hidden between two casinos. Trying to imagine how many couples had said their vows, stayed married and walked away with no regrets. She spotted one couple departing from the chapel, as the groom carried his newly wed bride through the double doors. Kissing romantically, as friends shred fresh flower petals. She smiled imagining what Gunnar is thinking. Closing her eyes, smelling her fresh bouquet of her two favorite flowers. Orchids and the flower of love, roses. Imagining in her busy mind how her groom to be looks like in his stunning black tailored tux.

He was almost finished prepping himself for a day he will always remember. Loosening his black tie, unbuttoning the last button on his coat and reaching for a dry martini. Sipping it slowly, enjoying his favorite cocktail, only cherishing martinis when he is in distress. Knowing this drink will certainly calm his nerves and loosen him up. Just a little and enough to ease his walk down memory lane. He smiled thinking to himself. He is finally marrying the girl of his dreams. Feeling a little guilty though. Knowing she has always wanted a fabulous wedding. With bridesmaids, live entertainment and people who she truly loves. Walking the room, eyeing the same view as Anna Maria he could clearly see couples, friends and many unfamiliar faces entering and exiting the overly crowed chapel. Is this how he wanted his wedding to be. He was not sure but would do anything for his soon to be beautiful bride. Knowing all she wanted was to marry him even if it would hurt many people's feelings mainly her father. He swallowed the last drop of liquid from his glass. Pouring himself a double this time. He felt warm, stunning and quite hyper. Pacing the room, reaching for his phone, seconds later releasing his warm hand from the handle and clearly changing his mind. Waiting for the right moment to call her. Knowing to give her more time to think and to see if her mind has changed about saying their vows in a strange and kind of bizarre city.

Her mind was racing. All of this has just been so sudden and now she feels unprepared for such a blissful ceremony. Still watching from her closed window. It was apparent hundreds of vows were said each day from this tiny chapel hidden between two casinos. Limos, fast cars, prostitutes and weird people were cruising and walking by. Witnessing all of this was a little overwhelming. She suddenly felt ill. A tear drop shed from her beautifully groomed eyes. Wondering if other brides have experienced the same pain, guilt and overwhelmed sense of doubt as she is having on her special day. Turning towards a chilled bottle of champagne for her and Gunnar to share after they have wed, she eyed it motionlessly. Reaching, pulling away and knowing she could no longer resist. She released the champagne cork silently into a damp cloth, no need for celebrating quite yet. Staring at the two glasses placed on a crystal platter. With no hesitation she grabbed on empty stem glass. She smiled as she has always loved the taste of sweet bubbling champagne. The coolness of the drink tickled her tongue and made her warm in the inside. Turning again to face the window where soon she and Gunnar will say their vows she giggled. Feeling a little more relaxed, knowing in her heart this is where she belongs.

He stared intensively at the line that was forming along the walkway, towards the front chapel doors. Wondering in his busy mind if the minister would be prompt, minutes or even hours behind. They were scheduled to say their vows in one hour. Couples were entering and leaving in a timely manner. Looking at his Rolex watch he timed one couple, then two and three. From start to finish, all in all each ceremony took less then fifteen minutes. One hundred and fifty dollars every fifteen minutes what a market. Thinking quick, multiplying how he was impressed by the gross amount of money the owners were making this day and every day.

He closed his eyes trying to comprehend the whole situation around him. Never did he have the desire to travel to Las Vegas, until yesterday evening. His father was a heavy gambler and lost enormous amounts of money playing hours of blackjack. Now he sees firsthand how overwhelming the city really can be. He never wanted to be like his father. All these years he has no love for gamblers and for the biggest gambling capital of the world, Las Vegas.

He shook his head gulping down his martini. Trying to ease bad memories of his father. With his dirty, vicious, bad habits and striving now for the fondest memories of his life. Marrying Anna Maria, the girl of his dreams. He smiled, knowing they will have a life filled with happiness, love and hopefully an abundance of children.

Anna Maria also never had any will to visit or vacation near this city, until now. Thinking in her mind the days her father was gone on business. Knowing now why he had spent many weekends here and never second guessing herself of the severity of her father's love to gamble. She smiled her mind was racing with many deep thoughts. Hurtful, pleasurable and secrets she had held in her mind for a very long time and never releasing them until now. Why now?

She turned, paced the room, while sipping in champagne. Again, facing the window to witness couples departing from the little white chapel.

Gunnar noticed the line to enter had slowly diminished. No longer was there a crowd. Just one couple lingering in front of the chapel's doors. Talking, holding hands and speaking in a calm way. He wondered if they were having second thoughts, as the way he was feeling at that very moment. This is not the way he had anticipated. He knew Anna Maria really wanted to marry in this city and he would honor her decision.

Staring at her watch she counted down the last remaining minutes. Sipping her last remaining liquid of champagne, grabbing her Channel handbag, tossing a mint in her mouth and hint of gloss on her lips. Reaching for the door knob her body trembled and suddenly stopped. She stood still, motionless and weak. She inhaled deeply looking up to the ceiling. Closing her eyes, she spoke wearily to herself. I'm I doing the right thing? Bowing her head forward, as soft tears streamed down her sad face.

She took a deep breath after being startled from a tapping on the door. Wiping fresh tears away she smiled. Realizing at that very moment soon she will be wed to the most handsome man alive. Slowly turning the doorknob, she quietly opened the door. He stood tall, arrogant and all alive with a gigantic smile lingering on his face. No words were spoken, just eyes of amazement. He handed her a bouquet of fresh roses. She stood still, as quiet as a calm night.

He finally spoke, 'You look ravishing.' He then leaned over and gave her a gentle kiss on her warm cheek. He sensed the weakness in her nerves. He has known her for some time. Believing in his mind something was not right by her deep expressions lying on her tender face.

She smiled, 'I love you.' Arching her head upward, moving close and kissing him vigorously.

Pulling away he said, Are you all right. Is this really what you want to do?'

She bowed her head forward smiling with no words releasing from her tender lips.

Well he said I do believe it is time. Extending his hand, she reached for him. Together they walked hand in hand down the steamy hallway. exiting through the front doors, facing the tiny white chapel

He swallowed hard, 'Are you sure this is what you want?'

'Of course.'

A lot was going through their minds. No need to speak, for they could read each other's vibes.

He sensed she had been drinking, from the way she stumbled a couple of times, to dodging small potholes on the sidewalk. She giggled like a little a girl every time she twisted her ankle. Laughing, strutting her stuff, still looking beautiful as ever, even though she was a little tipsy. She tried calmly to walk in her high heels.

He held her strong. A special glow appeared on her blushed face. Showing an expression like no other. She was truly beautiful in every way.

He spoke, 'Anna Maria' there will never be a dull moment whenever I'm with you.'

She giggled, 'Oh really.'

'Yes, really. You light up my world.' He stopped strong, bracing her petite body against his. Staring into her gazing, piercing eyes, 'I love you.' Seconds later, gentle engulfing her glossy lips. Releasing, smiling and winking in a mischievous way.

She laughed, 'What was that for?'

'You make me crazy. I cannot believe in the next few minutes we will be man and wife.'

Suddenly she appeared pale. He immediately sensed a new women.

She deeply inhaled, 'I really cannot believe it either and her face immediately saddened.'

He gently touched her hand and placed her soft palm on her cheek. Gently resting his hand on hers, moving his neck, gently kissing her fingers, sliding down her wrist back up again to her fingers. Nipping her fingertips, kissing her hand, closing his eyes smiling. Releasing minutes later entering though the double doors of the tiny chapel.

A young couple looking as if they were in their twenties stood face to face ready to say their own special vows. Both dressed in tattered jeans, sneakers and matching T-shirts with some rock group with an iron on logo pressed in the center of each back. Anna Maria watched intensively. Wondering in her mind if they knew exactly what they were doing. It looked as if this was just a spur of the moment thing to do. Prepping themselves for their special day certainly was not top of their list of things to do. What mattered was this couple seemed truly happy to Anna Maria. She smiled inhaling slowly. Looking in the groom's eyes as he slowly slipped her wedding ring on his bride's finger. Her eyes widened, mouth open and tears streamed heavily down her rosy cheeks. Within seconds no more whispers echoed in the tiny chapel, smiles turned to frowns and the bride laid helpless in her boyfriend's arms. No sign of being overheated or exhausted she had fainted. Minutes later opening her eyes, as a small group of people had surrounded her. Eyeing curiously wondering why she had collapsed.

'Oh my God,' vocalizing in total sorrow, she said, 'Gunnar I hope she is OK.'

He smiled, 'She will be fine. Just her nerves taking over. He also thought curiously in his mind. Is this the kind of wedding she really wanted.

The young woman finally spoke after many minutes. She said, 'Billy, I'm so sorry.'

He smiled there is a reason for everything. This day was not meant to be.

She kissed him romantically.

He extended his hand, reaching and pulling her close.

Applause was heard at the back of the room. A group of people cheered them on as if they had just wed. cheering in a way as if they had made the right decision and not marrying for the sake of saying they got married in Las Vegas.

Anna Maria stood frozen with her bouquet tightly pressing against her chest. Smiling at the young couple as they departed, sensing a whole new feeling of guilt, cheating and dishonesty.

Time had passed, hours turned in minutes within just a few seconds. Simultaneously they both walked up two steps. Instantly stopping and facing each other. Witnesses many ceremonies it had become routine in their minds. Knowing what to expect from the beginning to the end.

She turned, seeing her father's complexion, blinking harshly, knowing it was just her imagination. Visualizing in her mind of her father's dying eyes. Instantly feeling paralyzed, lost and selfish.

Hearing the pastor speak about ten seconds Gunnar interrupted. Speaking openly, ',Anna Maria why are we here?'

She rolled her shoulders.

'You know this is not what you want.'

Tears streamed down her cheeks, eyes fluttered, mouth moistened.

He smiled extending his hand whispering it is time to go.

With no hesitation she lunged forward, holding tightly, softly crying and saying, 'I love you.'

Frustrated, annoyed and surprised, the pastor threw his arms up in the air, shaking his head in disbelief.

She turned her head before exiting, 'I'm so sorry for Pastor Bob.'

He waved, taking a deep breath and calling out the next couple on his list. Praying silently this was not going to be strike three.

Hand in hand, exiting right before she tossed her bouquet landing in the lap of a woman sitting quietly in the pew. She looked up with an everlasting smile on her face.

Anna Maria giggled best of luck. She felt more alive than ever. Coming to the important conclusion life is not always fair. In the end living, loving, sacrifice and family is the most important gift of all.

'Gunnar,' she said.

'Yes.'

'I'm starving.'

He laughed, 'When aren't you. Follow me.'

A couple blocks he sighted a white limousine. Secretly hiring a driver for the entire evening. A special wedding gift for his wife. A wedding that never happened. In the end an extraordinary evening filled with love, surprises and above all a future wedding filled with family and friends. Not a little chapel sighted between two casinos. Next time their wedding will be in God's house.

In a cathedral in front of hundreds of people not strange or unfamiliar faces. The day filled with a priest, altar boys and church bells ringing peacefully in the background.

No words were spoken for the longest time. Their minds were busy. Did they make the right decision? Neither will ever know.

He placed her hand near his face. Gently kissing her forehead, staring into her glassy eyes, winking in a seductive way. Moving towards her lips, around her ears, slithering down her slender neck and engulfing her moistened mouth.

No resistance.

He was relentless.

She released her tension allowing him to take control.

He whispered, 'I love you.'

You do know we have company. I think we have an audience watching us. He reached for the window shade button. It was jammed. No closure tonight for privacy it lies in their hotel room.

The driver spoke, 'Hey man, sorry about the window. No one ever uses it.'

Gunnar winked softly saying just our luck.

She laughed.

He engulfed her neck for the last time, smiling, pulling away, straightening his shirt and tie.

Looking to her right she eyed cascading waterfalls. A beautiful and brilliant entrance to one of the most popular restaurants in Las Vegas.

Seconds later the limo pulled up in front of two bell men.

She smiled feeling very peaceful with herself, happy and sensing a great gift of hope for their lives together. A celebration not of marriage. Time will tell, but a great gift of how two people in love can devote their dream with friends and family and not secretly escaping just to inherit a worldwide business.

Sitting romantically, hidden in a corner, surrounded by tropical plants, fresh flowers, flickering candles and soft music playing in the background.

She hesitated, 'Gunnar do you think we made the right decision?'

'About what.'

You know are you disappointed in me. I'm sorry about today. Tears suddenly streamed down her blushed cheeks. 'I do love you.'

'Anna Maria, you do not need to explain anything to me.'

But I want to. 'I love you Gunnar. We should have been married. I do not understand why I bailed out. I clearly was a coward.'

He instantly reached for her hand. 'We do not need to rush into marriage. We love each other. Next time we will take it nice and slow. We will know the date, time and place. One very special day.'

She looked into his eyes bowing down.

Lifting her chin proud he spoke sincerely. 'You are the most beautiful, gracious and bravest woman I have ever known. Do not ever let me hear you again say you are weak and a coward. We both made the right decision on walking out. We are a team and we will always stick together.'

She paused, 'I love you.'

'You are not selfish and that is why I love you. You made a very important decision. I know how difficult it was for you. If you did not care we would have been married hours ago, but you have a warm heart. You love your father deeply. His spirit would be haunting you for the rest of your life if we just disappeared and never told a soul about our adventure. Sneaking into marriage and feeling much guilt. This is not how you imagined your wedding would be. You have always wanted to look like a princess. I am allowing you to have your dream wedding even if your father does not deny his dying wish. Our time will come.

She smiled, wiping a fresh tear from her lower lip. She paused, 'I hate to even bring it up, but what about Antonio?'

'I have it all worked out. We need to pray your father stays strong and not give up. He needs to hear all, before his eyes release into total darkness. There is no more hiding and running away from Antonio. He has messed with the wrong family. His time is up and soon he will never be heard of again.'

She sat listening, feeling protected and wanted.

'Anna Maria', he said, 'I promise you we have a bright and big future ahead of us. Everything is going to be all right'. He leaned forward giving her the sweetest kiss ever winking, 'Don't you ever forget.'

For hours they acted like newlyweds, kissing, holding and eyeing one another with glazing eyes. Acting as if this was the first time they have ever touched, kissed and made love. Hours of passionate role playing. Steamy showers, warm and erotic sex. Teasing each other, engulfing tender spots and seeking unstoppable foreplay.

She nearly had enough. Her body hot as she lay still as the night, fading slowly into darkness. Fighting hard to keep her tired eyes open, no use.

He watched her intensively. So lovely a person with beautiful features and a heart strong as a cold winter night. A fighter and a lover. Who could ask for more? Smiling sliding his fingertips against her cheek bone, slithering down her neck. Gentle swaying across her soft nipples. He just loved to watch her, as the shadows of the candles flickering enhanced her prominent features. An elegant body with a womanly shape. He kissed her breast, touching licking gently, staring at her closed lids. Wondering if she would ever wake. Wanting to engulf her and please her to no end. He whispered, 'Anna Maria.'

She moaned lying still.

'Anna Maria, I want you.'

She smiled never releasing her tight closed lids.

He slowly moved his legs between her loose thighs. Arching high, touching his body against hers, moving up and down, side to side. Feeling more aroused than ever.

Teasing, playfully licking, entering. Warm, hard and tight. Slowly steadily releasing shifting inward.

Insomnia no more. She could no longer lie still. Playfully swaying with each rhythmical move. A vibrant tempo, one routinely played and acted out.

No resistance, her body danced with each beat and fluttered.

He whispered, 'I love you. Rest, later this is our last evening together. I want you for all myself.'

Pulling upward, softly releasing sensual words she spoke, 'Gunnar, after tonight you will never want to leave this room.''

He smiled eyeing her tender lips. I wonder what our really honeymoon will be like.'

She laughed, 'I cannot wait.' Leaning upward she attacked him. Kissing vigorously, dancing her tongue against his, gliding her fingers down the back of his spine. Rolling over allowing him to take over. She smiled knowing she is a woman who has it all. Closing her eyes slowly and peacefully breathing in his scent. Enjoying the last few hours before their splendid night comes to a quick end.

She smiled in her sleep. Knowing love is patient and kind. Gunnar will be the man she will wake up to every morning for the rest of her beautiful life, with the man she has always loved.

Chapter 19

Her body trembled. Cold breeze filtered her childhood room, not wanting to lie alone anymore. She was madly in love. No longer did she want to wake up every morning with emptiness. This playing and acting from her father needed to stop. She spent hours thinking of where she and Gunnar must rest. Should she stay in the mansion with Rosie or escape to his little hideaway on the south side.

A terrible thought triggered Antonio. She intensively searched in her mind a way to delete him from the family. She knew Gunnar already had plans for his disappearance, but still she feared him. Knowing now how evil he really is. Could he hurt her, Gunnar and even her father who dearly adores him? Her mind was racing with disturbing thoughts, hardcore thoughts of hatred. She was alarmed by a man who betrayed and played with innocent women's minds and precious lives. Wondering how one human being could be so cold and unpredictable. Conning his whole life and retrieving everything all these beautiful women have worked hard for.

Closing her eyes, she inhaled deeply. Looking towards the window, eyeing the beautiful blue sky, she looked up softly speaking, 'Please give me the strength to move forward. I need to not to fear Antonio and have him fear me. Let me live as I should. I dearly pray my father believes my true words. Please free my father from his pain and peacefully send him above the gates of Heaven. Carrying him to my mother's side and let them both rest in a new beautiful world. Filled with miraculous people and beautiful angels guarding their every move. I'm grateful for my life who all shares with me. Please I'm begging you. Amen.'

She smiled minutes later walking through the mansion doors. She immediately felt the cool breeze penetrate against her exposed skin as she inhaled fresh dew in the morning air.

Each step she came closer to her father, which seemed like days of agony and defeat. The halls smelled again of wet dog, ammonia and stale pee. Coughing in the palm of her hands she entered slowly and cautiously. First feeling the coldness and then emptiness of his room. He smiled for the first time in days.

Her heart sank. Immediately she launched forward, holding him. Tears streamed down her chilled cheeks. She knew this was just the beginning of faith and endless prayers. Hoping her dreams appear to come true.

She whispered, 'Daddy, I love you.'

His aching arms held her tight.

'I'm so sorry what you have gone though. Forgive me for the bad and I'm deeply blessed to have you in my world.' No longer did she shed tears nor pain. Her father has always been her hero and in her gracious precious life.

Struggling to speak he whispered, 'Anna Maria my baby girl. Where have you been. Your beautiful face says all. You are truly happy aren't you.'

Fresh wet tears welled up in her swollen eyes. All she could do was shake her head smiling as water dripped down her rosy cheeks. Her vision became blurred and she saw the light in her father's prominent dark brown eyes.

Bending forward she gave him a precious honest kiss.

He reached for her smiling for the first time in days.

She whispered, 'Daddy, are you all right?'

'Yes, baby girl, everything is all right.' Kissing the palm of her hand smiling as his eyelids slowly sealed into darkness.

She stroked the side of his face.

He smiled, never releasing the soft pressure of his cuffed hands and loving her tender touch.

He vaguely whispered, 'Anna Maria, I love you. Please talk to me. I have missed your beautiful voice.'

'Shall I read?'

'No tell me about him.'

Startled by his behavior she stood frozen.

'Go ahead,' he said.

'Daddy, are you sure?'

He bowed smirking.

'Daddy you will love him. Trust me his name is—'

Before she could even say Gunnar McKay, her worst nightmare had just trashed his bold body through the hospital room doors. Trailing behind in disgust a kind and disturbed nurse spoke loudly. 'Miss Cecola I am truly sorry. I told this gentleman no visitors and only family members allowed to enter and see Mr. Cecola. Would you like him dismissed immediately?

'Thank you I can handle him'.

'If you need anything, please ring. I will be waiting.'

Turning to face the door he glared viciously straight into her eyes. Antonio spoke abruptly, 'I am family.'

With no hesitation Anna Maria fired back.' Like hell you are. You will never be family.'

He paused, 'I clearly do not understand. What on earth has gotten into you. Why are you acting crazy?'

'I'm not crazy.'

He smiled, 'I know you are not crazy. You are crazy in love with me.'

Vomit rolled the lining of her mouth. She wanted to exhale and release all the hatred she has for him. Instead she faced her tired, grieving and sick father.

She felt his tension rise from the grip of his palm.

Bending near his ear she whispered, 'Daddy, I promise you no one will ever destroy my life or Cecola & Gold. I learned it all from you. Daddy I'm begging you to release Antonio. We will talk later. Evil lurks your way. Beware for he will con you like he has others. If you have never trusted or honored me before, please listen and listen well. I want him destroyed before he destroys you. I have men monitoring his every move. You will never be alone. Do not listen to his words and please be careful. Remember one false move and you maybe history.'

His eyes widened. He felt fear. Never has he ever been threatened, or afraid of anyone. He knew his daughter well. Tension was rising in the room. Acting quickly, he pulsed his fingers against her soft skin. He winked releasing his swollen eyes shut.

She sat staring at her beloved role model, never losing sight of him. Thinking in her mind how to get rid of Antonio.

Startled by the twitching of his fingertips she sat calmly. Waiting patiently for his next move and wondering what tricks play in his head. She deeply knew her father well. Well enough to know he was perturbed by her true words of dishonesty, betrayal and a man who had con him for months. He felt nausea, weak and used. His body ached, blurry speech, as well as his mind depleting. He thought long and hard wondering if he was well and sharp. If he would have ever been taken advantage of. Was he really his weakness of life, or has he met his match for the very first time.

He spoke softly, 'Is he still here?'

'Yes.'

'Baby girl please be careful. I will call in my men.'

She smiled, 'Thank you.'

They have always protected him and loves the Cecola family deeply.

Mr. Cecola's fine men of many years have learned tremendous about Antonio's ruthless lifestyle. Their ways of getting rid of him was different from Anna Maria's. She wanted him to suffer and not disappear. She thought he deserved to rot in hell and live day to day in a violent world, as he did to others.

Mr. Cecola spoke quietly, 'I need for him to be arrested and sent away.'

'Daddy, now is not the time. We need a few more days to get all details together.'

She whispered. 'Daddy he is waiting patiently for you. What should I do?'

Inhaling deeply, he spoke, 'Please go now. You must disappear.'

What she said. 'Daddy what about your wish, your demands. Who will run Cecola & Gold?'

'Just go. There is not time to talk.'

'Daddy I need to know. Please tell me.'

'You must listen.'

She cried, 'Daddy, time is running out.'

'Everything will be all right trust me,' he scolded, 'Go now.'

She stood weak, frantic and nervous, wondering in her cold mind if she would inherit or lose it all to someone unknown.

'Please baby girl. I will tell Antonio you need some time to be alone.'

Waving his palm towards his side. He came walking over.

Mr. Cecola you are looking well today. Can I get you anything?

He shook his head smiling with a disguise. Reaching for his hand he extended his. Hand in hand they eyed each other for the longest time.

Anna Maria did as her father said with flowing amounts of tears welling up in her eyes. She was not happy, but she knew she had no choice and her father was right.

Antonio smiled, reaching for her.

No response, remorse or expression of kindness flittered her stone cold, hurtful face.

Mr. Cecola finally spoke, 'I'm worried about Anna Maria. She has been acting crazy lately. You will not be hearing from her for some time.'

He curiously watched him. 'Where is she going?'

Smiling he spoke far away. 'To a place which will heal her. As you can tell she needs help. Anna Maria is weak. I think you have been noticing her bizarre behavior lately, as well as others.'

He hesitated, 'Has she agreed to get help?'

'I believe she has no choice.'

He was playing the part and smiling on the inside, showing no remorse no expression. 'Please do not fail me. Right now, I really need your support.'

Antonio had no clue what just had happened, but he did know this. He now had all the power. The power to take over Cecola & Gold, disappear and never be heard of again. He though was curious where Anna Maria was going. Why had she agreed to go to away? Was it the money she wanted or something else? Soon he will find out.

'Antonio, my son.'

He smiled.

'Be strong in power, for I'm too weak to carry on. I'm counting on you.'

He released his sweaty palm, walking away, smiling as if he conquered his goal.

Eying him with one slightly eye opened Michael Cecola took a deep breath. Releasing all tension exhaling. Watching him disappear, his mind wandered. Wondering what the hell is going to happen. He feared for Anna Maria. Closing his eyes, raising his hand to the Lord, he read a silent prayer

Our father,

Who art in Heaven,

hallowed be thy name,

thy kingdom come,

thy will be done

on Earth as

it is in Heaven.

give us this day

our daily bread

and forgive us our

trespasses

as we forgive those that trespass against us,

and lead us not

into temptation,

but deliver us

from evil

Amen.

Give me strength Lord for I believe my time is running out. I need to know my daughter is well before I take my last breath of fresh air. Please I'm begging you, forgive me for all bad I've done. You are the creator of this world. I have always believed and soon I will be with you. Do not take my life right now. I have one wish before I die. Clearly, I hope you understand. Anna Maria deserves happiness. May you bring peace to her heart.

His weak body was slowly shutting down. He fell back to sleep and the next time he raised his eyelids was past midnight. He fought hard to remain still, as a shadowy figure entered slowly, silently and cautiously. Immediately his tired eyes felt as if someone had stapled them wide open. Breathing heavily, he could feel his heartbeat triple in rhythm. Was this the end. Who was coming near? Soon he would find out.

'Mr. Cecola please do not be alarmed. I'm truly sorry to disturb you at such an odd hour. I need for you to listen. You do know who I am.'

He extended his hand towards him for the very first time, waiting patiently for a response.

Minutes seemed to go by eventually their palms met.

He spoke brokenly, 'Gunnar right.'

'Yes sir.'

'I have been waiting for you. Please forgive me. We have no time to talk, for Anna Maria comes first. I know you love my daughter, as she loves you. Did you talk to her today and did she express how concerned I was for her?'

'Yes.'

'I want her closely watched day and night.'

'Where do you want me to take her?'

He whispered, 'Far away and please watch your back.' He then pulled his cuffed hands near Gunnar's face. Arching forward he kissed his knuckles. Whispering be careful. 'You must go.'

Gunnar spoke silently thank you. 'I love your daughter very much. I need to ask you one thing. It is very important.'

His eyes were fluttering and fighting hard to see with his slightly closed eyes.

'Mr. Cecola I would like your permission, for I want to marry your daughter. I love her very much and will take great care of her.'

No response.

He became quiet, still, losing holding of his soft grip against Gunnar's hand.

'Gunnar whispered please Mr. Cecola answer me.'

Still no movement or signs of awareness. He felt numb. Lost and worried. Wondering if he did hear his true words of marriage or blacking out, for he has no desire for his special daughter to wed.

Mr. Cecola please I need to know.

Once Gunnar figured out, he was not coherent, he slowly departed feeling overwhelmed. Gunnar studied hard in his busy mind wondering if Mr. Cecola truly wants

Antonio gone and put away, or another game he must play. Does he really honor me for who I am, and does he feel I am the right man for his girl. Shall he trust him for all the evil he has created? Soon he will find out. He will take Anne Maria somewhere far away and no one will ever find out, where to rest, until the day she finds peace.

Chapter 20

'You know you should not be here he whispered.'

She smiled, 'I know.'

'We should be hiding.'

'We are she chuckled.'

'No, we are not.'

She laughed, 'There is not place I rather be.' Smiling. 'You know me better than anyone. I could never think about hiding anywhere else.'

'You worry me.'

'Why worry.'

'Why worry you need to be protected.'

She continued to smile, as if she had never smiled in days.

Thinking to himself. He was truly concerned still believing Mr. Cecola was playing mind games with him. After all he has done. Why must he trust him for all the harm he has done. Was this all a setup, or a cold stone father who wants forgiveness before he takes his last final breath. Will he destroy his last wish for his daughter and honor her longing gift of marriage? Could there be a chance he does not believe us and still trusts Antonio. Is he playing with our heads?

Gunnar continued to deliberate in his mind what were his options. Run and hide like Mr. Cecola or keep her where she is. Does Mr. Cecola fear Antonio as he appears to?

Gunnar deeply prayed for Mr. Cecola's honesty and trust. Wanting this man to destroy all the hatred he has ever had for him and take him as his one and only son.

She smiled, 'What are you thinking?'

'Your eyes say it all. I know you better than that. It is as busy as a calculator.'

He laughed. 'I guess you are right.'

'Well what is it?'

He hesitated, reaching for her hand. 'Anna Maria, I love you so much. I just do not want you to get hurt. We have no idea how crazy Antonio really is. We learned he has stolen many innocent women's lives. He is corrupt, changed his identity many times, robbed and has been in and out or prison for many years. This tells a lot about someone. Who knows what else he has done.? With his track record it would not surprise me if he has men working for him to do his dirty work. He is very sneaky, cunning, arrogant and murder is probably hidden on his rap sheet.

She swallowed hard, 'Murder?'

'Yes.'

Suddenly a mad rush of blood flowing through her veins. She gasped, 'Gunnar my father.'

'What about your father.'

'I'm scared. What if he harms him?'

He , 'I am wondering the same thing. I believe he will not harm to your father.'

'Why.'

'Antonio wants Cecola & Gold. Why would he harm your father if in his will there are no documents to clarify he would be president? I thought only verbally you and your father have talked. No written explanation just words and no will.'

She did not want to say what slipped out of her sealed lips, but the words just seem to sail out. 'What if he lied?'

'Well, then we have a serious problem.'

He paused for the longest time. 'Anna Maria, do you think your father is lying or telling the truth?'

She eyed him curiously, 'About what?'

'You know' allowing me to be in your life and honoring me to take your hand in marriage.'

She smiled, 'I believe my father.'

'What makes you so sure he is telling the truth?'

She leaned over giving him a sweet, tender kiss whispering in his ears.

He fawned raising one eyebrow.

'You said it earlier these eyes tell all.'

He smiled arching forward, kissing her outer right eyes. Whispering in her ear, 'You know you have the most precious, mysterious and beautiful eyes of all. They sparkle with a curious twist to them. You light up my life with your dazzling eyes, brilliant smile and a contagious laugh. I love you. I loved you the first day I laid eyes on you. I truly never believed you would not fall for me.'

'Why would you say such a thing?'

'You know why.'

'Is it because how I was raised? My father's power and money.'

'Bingo.'

'Well you certainly thought wrong. She smiled I never told you this before, but I used to watch you all the time. I should say every day. Every time I closed my eyes a vision of your beautiful body pondered in my mind. I admired you and found you to be very attractive. From the moment I closed my eyes in the evening you seem to reminisce in my mind. I could not stop thinking about you.'

He did not say a word enjoying her little tale of meeting Mr. Right.

Reaching, breathing deeply, speaking erotically into his ear.' I had planned our little collision all along.'

He laughed, 'You did what?'

'You heard me.'

'Why have you never told me this before.'

'I do not know. I did not think it was important. You see I wanted you so bad and I knew you were the right man for me. By your grace, attitude and above all slight arrogance of great confidence.'

'You think I am arrogant.'

She giggled in a good way.

'You could have just said hello.'

'I was nervous. My blood raced every time you jogged near. I watched you for weeks and then had the courage to collide into you.'

He laughed, 'I felt horrible. You did not move for the longest time. I thought I had to call in the medics.

She giggled, 'Look where we are today. My plan worked.

'Yes, but I bet you would never believe we would be where we are today.'

She smiled, 'No.'

'Why cannot our life be simple like normal people.'

She smiled, 'Soon my love have patience.'

With no hesitation he exhaled, 'My patience has gone. Believe me I'm taking no more shit from anyone. I should have stood up to your father. Fight like a man and maybe our lives would be simple and pleasant. I was weak, bitter and alone.'

'You also feared my father like many others. I never wanted to believe who my father is or who he had become. Now I know. He portrays two lives. One life in our mansion, as a father and a friend. A gentle caring man and another only a few have been a part off. A secret world filled of gambling, hatred, evil and cold disturbing words I hate to release from my mouth. Deep down I do not want to believe my father has anything to do with the dirty mob'.

He saw fear and gentle tears swelled in her prominent eyes. Reaching for her she whispered, 'Gunnar, please never leave me.'

He felt sick to his stomach from all the pain he has caused. He could no longer hide his emotions. With a shaky voice he said, 'Anna Maria, I will never leave you again. I love you. I hope you can forgive me someday.'

She smiled resting her head against his. 'What is in the past is over. The future holds bright for the two of us. No one ever will come between us again. Even if we run and hide. Hide in another country just to survive. Plan two identities just like innocent victims trying to find peace. For they have been taken advantage of and just want to be left alone. All alone in a secret place surrounded by beauty and miles of seclusion.'

He watched her from the corner of his eye.

'I know you think I'm crazy, but I am not. I just want to be happy, left alone and live my life as I shall. I would not think twice about boarding a plane and leaving everything behind.'

He eyed her, .What about Rosie?'

Her eyes welled up with fresh tears. She spoke softly, 'I will miss her deeply but believe me she will survive.' She half grinned, 'I just maybe might bring her with us.' Pausing briefly, she spoke openly. 'Remember she is strong, courageous and the only person who will fight like hell to keep me from escaping and leaving my home of many years.'

He held her chin up. Staring at her for the longest time. He finally spoke, 'Our life will be normal soon just as it was in the beginning. No madness, false hopes and separation. We belong together. '

She smiled bowing her head against his chest. 'I believe every word you say,' closing her eyes, daydreaming.

Pulling slowly away he leaned forward. Lifting her legs around his arm, gripping and carrying her up among the spiral stairs. Reaching the loft, entering slowly he gently placed her tender body on a pile of flush pillows.

She smiled.

Placing a down comforter softly around her relaxed body he whispered in her ear. 'Wait here I will be back.'

Closing her eyes, she whispered, 'I'm not going anywhere. This is where I belong.'

Before exiting the double doors, he stared at his beautiful princess. Silently praying God will honor his wish, for life with Anna Maria would be the most precious gift of all. He continued to watch her, as if this was her last breath. Remembering in his mind the evening he had deserted her. All alone in the mist of the night. Watching her intensively he sat near her side. Tenderly swaying his fingers up and down the sides of her soft cheeks. He wanted to hide, but deep down he had to run. Run away from evil. Evil as in men who have no remorse for their terrible actions. Cruel men and one leader who will do anything to get their way, even if it shall endanger one's lives. His own life. His mind was rewinding. Ticking back to the past. A past he deeply wanted to erase. Shaking his head and tightly closing his eyes. He tried deeply to forget about that painful night. He just could not escape the cruel behavior playing in his head, like a broken record skipping and moving ahead. At midnight he placed an envelope near her side. Kissing her tender face, disappearing in the quiet night, without a trace. Never turning back and never saying why. He still wonders in his mind if he truly has won her broken heart back. Deep down he believes from her precious ways. To how her smile rises each time he enters the room.

Blinking away the past, smiling, he bent down giving her the sweetest kiss. Exiting and never releasing his eyes from her petite body, until he was inches behind her bedroom. Walking down the spiral stairs, reminiscing quiet thoughts of a peaceful pray of dreams and solitude. He knew he had to plan a big take down. His worst enemy, Antonio. Father Cecola can wait, for he is weak and incoherent. He closed his eyes praying for forgiveness for all the bad he had done and for what may occur in the future. Knowing soon he will be in the peak of the storm, fighting for his future and life. Wanting life to be fresh and pure, as it was in the beginning with the most beautiful woman who walks this earth.

He sat motionless facing the chilled northern waters, as if the calm before the storm. Feeling uneasy, as if a strange presence was over watching every move. He turned towards the patio doors. From the corner of his eyes he noticed his Mercedes Benz car door was slightly opened. Cautiously entering the open house, he focused on the upper loft where Anna Maria was resting. He darted up the stairs grabbing a pottery vase placed on a corner end table. Fearfully inching the bedroom door open. Moving slowly and quietly coming inches from her side. He felt relieved in a way. Whispering as he covered her mouth with the strength of his hand. Saying do not move or say a word. Someone is here.

Her tired eyes sprung open wide and alert. She listened to his words. Slowly moving quietly and following his body movement.

Releasing her mouth, he whispered, 'Anna Maria, Antonio must know we are here.'

Her eyes welled up with fresh tears. 'How do you know.'

'Everything is too quiet, as if the wild had vanished into the dense woods. You know what I mean. I learned it all from you. I sense trouble. We must leave right away. I need to check my car first. Please be quiet and follow me. There maybe one or more men. I have no idea. So please listen to me.'

Her heart was pounding as fast as it could beat. She was sweating with fear. Fear of what would happen. Her mind was racing with disturbing thoughts. Who would want to hunt them? Her sanctuary, home from away home. Why must this all be happening, she swallowed hard.

Gripping her hand, he quietly spoke, 'We must leave.'

'Gunnar, do we have to. Are you sure about this? Do you really think Antonio found us?'

Placing his fingertip against his lips he whispered, 'Sss, we cannot take a chance. Do you sense an eerie unwanted feeling surrounding the premises.'

She did not speak. Closing her eyes and inhaling the crisp air of fresh pine. Opening her eyes slowly, observing the quietness of the call of the wild. Eyeing the view of the crisp blue water, looking towards the open skies, she inhaled deeply.

Turning his head, he eyed her curiously. Wondering what thoughts were racing in her mind.

Feeling not troubled but free, half smiling. Sensing a warm feeling. A beautiful emotion one she has always felt in her warm heart whenever her special friend was near. She was near. There was no doubt in her mind. Within seconds a shadowy silhouette appeared from the horizon. Why had she just appeared. Was she warning us or saying her friendly hello? Anna Maria watched intensively, as this beautiful creature darted openly above them. Swooping, diving and circling the territory where they cautiously stood. Screeching and within seconds disappearing in the dense woods.

Moving slowly, eyeing one another, breathing deeply Anna Maria inhaled breathlessly. Swallowing hard, seeing not one, but two shadowy figures. Wondering in her mind if there are more foreigners and what are they doing on her property which leads down a bumpy and dusty shallow road at least a mile stretch. Not many people know about this secluded inlet. Once near the end of the road they seem to always head back in a timely manner. If one does not know this hidden destination they are spooked in an instant by the deep and dense woods. Sounds of the wild and a feel of an unwanted presence lurking from behind. Never has the Cecola family ever heard or seen any motor vehicles down near their path or private lake. Anna Maria's mind was racing. Racing with disturbing thoughts. Thoughts of disbelief and thoughts of invasion. Her hidden lake has just been invaded. Her favorite getaway is no longer hidden only overtaken by unwanted people lurking around. She clearly knows that only about thirty people have visited Glory Lake, family and very close friends.

Chills shivered down her spine, she whispered, 'Gunnar.'

Glancing towards her with fear in his eyes he spoke, 'Please follow my moves.'

With no hesitation she let him lead the way. Trembling as if she would collapse from fear, an overwhelming feeling of exhaustion, thirst and death.

'Anna Maria.'

Her prominent eyes moistened still sensing fear inches away.

'Anna Maria,' she heard his voice scratching and deep.

Still gleaming at Gunnar, she spoke shakily, 'I recognize the voice.'

'Who is he?'

'I'm not sure, but I do know his voice well.'

'What do you want to do Anna Maria?'

She paused for the longest time. She eventually spoke, 'Vinnie his name is Vinnie.'

'What?' Gunnar said.

'One of the men here is Vinnie. A very good friend of my father's'

'Do you like and trust him?'

'Yes,' as wet tears streamed done her naked face.

'What are you going to do? Or what are we going to do?'

She half smiled, 'I'm fond of this man. He has been a family friend now for many years. I do trust him.'

Gunnar replied, 'Are you sure?'

'Trust me on this one.'

She spoke softly, 'Vinnie.' Holding Gunnar's cold hand, she walked slowly towards Vinnie and clearly seeing who was be at his side, Johnny.

Releasing hold of Gunnar. Lunging for Vinnie she gently sobbed, 'Vinnie' what are you doing here. You scared me to death.'

Standing still, calm, never releasing words from his sealed lips Gunnar listened intently. Wanting so badly to interrupt. He kept cool and still as one of the quietest winter's night he smiled.

Moments later Vinnie and his partner reached their right hand towards Gunnar.

'Oh, I'm truly sorry.' Smiling she openly spoke, 'Gunnar, this is Vinnie and Johnny.'

At the same time, they spoke, 'Gunnar, it is a pleasure to meet you. We have heard all about you.'

He left eye twitched expressing a concern look on his frazzled face. 'Really?' Gunnar replied.

Yes.

Arching one eyebrow, he suddenly asked, 'How do you know me?'

'Oh, I guess you have never met Rosie,' Vinnie chuckled.

Half weary eyed Gunnar spoke, 'Not officially, no, I have not met Rosie. Just short hellos and secret goodbyes. I assure you I do know she is one hell of a lady. She raised a beautiful, brave and gracious woman.'

Anna Maria smiled wide as if she were on cloud nine. She again said, 'What are you guys doing here?'

Johnny smiled, 'Your beautiful Rosie told us everything. She pretty much barracked and locked us in the mansion. Of course, she made us spaghetti and meatballs, fresh bread, salad and served us a couple bottles of red wine. She had it all worked out. Turning the alarm system on as soon as we marched through the doors. Serving us a homemade meal and desperately trying to intoxicate us. She at one time choked up about her life in the mansion and living with the Cecola family. She truly loves you all very much. We believe every word she had said from Mr. Cecola's behavior and wrong decision about Anna Maria and Antonio.'

She inhaled deeply, 'Thank you.'

Gunnar kept quiet and cool listening intently, patiently and eager to hear what they had to say about him.

Anna Maria spoke shakily, 'Did Rosie say anything about Antonio?'

'Yes, we are here to protect you.'

'What do you mean protect?'

'Last night Rosie spent hours talking. She eventually spoke fearfully about Antonio. We deeply became concerned knowing deep down she was right about Antonio. Rosie is a bright woman. I have never disobeyed, dishonored or show any disrespect towards her. I believe everything she has ever said from her youngest years up to now. Everyone loves her deeply and she will always be a Cecola. One sad day she will die a saint, rise above the gates of Heaven and watch over us. She truly will be our guardian angel, as we will have her soul resting in our beating hearts.'

She smiled again, 'Thank you. I never knew how much everyone cared so deeply for her. You know she did a lot of talking in Spanish when all the guys were around.'

'Yes, she would always spank my hands every time I reached for her fresh bread. It was apparent she did not like our loudest, crude behavior or language. He chuckled when all the guys were ready to leave her hugs were warm, tight and strong. It was as if it was the last time that she would ever see us again.'

Every time Anna Maria reminisced in her mind about Rosie she just smiled. Giggling in the inside as if she were a little girl again.

Johnny reached out to Anna Maria, 'Has Antonio ever been here before or knows where Glory Lake is?'

'He has never been here before, and I hope he never finds out,' she smirked, 'By the way, how did you know where I was?'

'Anna Maria please where else would you be.'

She smiled, 'You are right. Where else would I be?'

Eventually after many minutes of conversing Gunnar half coughed, 'May I step in and say something?'

Vinnie bowed his head, 'Of course.'

'Do you two really know all about Antonio and how he is trying to swindle his way into Cecola & Gold?'

'Rosie did ramble on a bit. Hearing enough to come and protect both of you.'

Gunnar inhaled deeply, 'I really think you need to hear more, and it will not be easy.'

Glancing towards the back of the house her eyes led towards the back and through the patio doors. All men followed with no hesitation.

Opening a bottle of Italian white wine, she smiled. Seeking from a distance a quick glance into Gunnar's overly, strained, tired and weathered eyes.

He smiled raising his head, winking in a devious way.

Gunnar spoke openly saying all he knew about Antonio. He inhaled deeply explaining nervously about his disruptive childhood, obedience adolescent years, and corrupted mind. Eventually taking a breather and walking to the refrigerator for another cold brew. His mind was wandering with deep and disturbing thoughts. Praying Antonio's greedy, dirty and ravishing lifestyle would soon come to a complete end. Trying hard to believe in his busy mind Antonio has no clue about him and Anna Maria, but he believes different. Closing his tired eyes. He continued to pray silently. He half smiled, as if Antonio was plastered and exploited all over the news and front page of every news stand. Wanting desperately for him to be captured and put away before a massive manhunt begins. Knowing there really is not much time especially if he detects any strange behavior from the Cecola family.

Eyeing Johnny, Gunnar swallowed hard, 'Please tell me is Mr. Cecola all right?

'Yes, is he.'

'How can you be sure?'

'Did you forget we work for him? During our conversation dinner with Rosie we made our calls. He was well protected. The hospital building is surrounded by men inside and out.'

Anna Maria said, 'I have faith in all of you, but I do not trust Antonio. I'm really scared. What if he is playing mind games with us? We need to get back to Daddy and the city like right now. I fear for Daddy's life. Not only because of Antonio, but he may pass at any time. I need to be by his side.'

Johnny smiled, 'Lead the way.'

Within minutes the lake house was all locked and secured, as if no one had ever entered through the doors in years.

Anna Maria smiled, arching her head and seeing the most beautiful creature leading her way. Feeling a warm sensation piercing her warm heart. She closed her worn out eyes and peacefully daydreamed of a woman who loves her deeply. Her gracious mother, Mary Catherine.

Chapter 21

Minutes ticked slowly by, turning into dreadful hours. Anna Maria was losing patience. Her mind was racing with thoughts of despair and disbelief.

She whispered, 'Daddy, why are you not waking up. I need you to open your eyes. I'm here patiently waiting. Please, Daddy I'm begging you.'

No movement or no strong pulse.

He looked as if his world had already ended, cold, pale and frail. One overly large monitor near his side. Tubes connected from the top of his head to his bruised colored toes.

Anna Maria continued to watch her beloved father. Closing her eyes and daydreaming of how once a man he really was. In her mind a genius. She truly loves him more and more as each minute slowly passes by. No matter what wrong the public has said about him. He is her father, good or bad. One man who knows what life is about, money, power and above all love. He is a very religious man who believed God gave their family strength. Especially when he lost his beautiful wife. Never missing mass and continuing to believe in the holy spirit. Praying nightly before he closes his blinds and falls into a deep sleep. Each morning waking up early, as he looks up to the sky thanking God. Thinking to himself how precious life really is and how he truly loves his family and friends. Once he has welcomed you into the Cecola family there is no rewinding back. A commitment of trust, loyalty, love and a great respect for all who are always invited back to the Cecola home. The ones he loves hold strong in his heart forever and ever.

Anna Maria smiled reminiscing in her drained, overworked, busy mind about her father. Praying soon he soon will open his tired eyes. Believing he will bless her dreams of marriage to Gunnar and overlook his verbal commitment of life together with Antonio.

She quietly stood up leaning over his frail body. Giving him the sweetest kiss on his swollen right cheek. Reaching for a warm blanket, she smiled.

'Anna Maria, I love you baby girl.'

She silently gasped for air, 'Oh Daddy.

'Pretty girl how long you been here?'

'Oh, not long, but I do love to watch you sleep. Wondering what dreams dance in your busy head.'

He half chuckled, 'If only you knew.'

She whispered, 'I would love to hear what you dream about. Am I in your deep dreams?'

'Always my love. You float through the air like a magical angel. Smiling as if you had no care in the world. Saying, Daddy, I will always love you. Look at me. I can fly. Saying someday I will sail up high in the sky and see Mom. We will be together again. Oh, I will never forget what she looks like. Beautiful with long dark hair, greenest of green eyes, tan skin and a continuous smile that never ends.'

Tears were streaming down her cheeks, beautiful wet and honest teardrops.

'No need to cry. This is my favorite dream of all.'

She smiled, 'Thank you'.

'Thank you for what.'

'For being my father. I love you.'

Bending over she cradled her father the best she could. Minutes later releasing his tender touch. Watching his every move and wondering if he was well enough to converse.

'Anna Maria, I do know you have a lot on your mind.'

'Yes, Daddy I do.'

With no hesitation she released her hidden words. 'Daddy I do not love Antonio. I literally despise him. He is not the man you think he is. Believe me he is more than just a convict. One man cannot be more troublesome than he. I love Gunnar McKay. I have always and will love him forever. My heart is no longer cold, but warm and fuzzy. He treats me like a princess just like you have'. She paused for a few minutes staring in another direction.

He slowly laid his palm on her hand whispering, 'Continue.'

She smiled, 'Gunnar and I flew to Las Vegas. We stood face to face on the altar reading each other's mind. We departed with smiles on our faces. While standing near Gunnar. I knew it was wrong. He sensed it all along and knew I wanted a family wedding with you by my side. Giving me away to the man I deeply love.'

He spoke shakily, 'Anna Maria thank you. You will receive your wish. A wedding, and I will be by your side.'

Wet tears continue to flow, as she hugged her father deeply. 'Thank you, Daddy. I do love you.'

'Tell me something. What or who changed your mind.'

He grinned, 'Good old Rosie. Also, the fear in your eyes whenever you mentioned his name. I'm so sorry. I know my baby girl. I clearly was denying your feelings and fear of this man. No need to worry. Antonio soon will be in the past and out of our lives.'

'So, you know about Antonio.'

'Yes, and clearly more.'

She swallowed hard thinking in her mind what her father has heard about Antonio. Could he be a murderer? At this point all she could think about is her frail, dying, beloved father and tune out all garbage about Antonio. Evil has no kind word to even express about this humane of a human being.

Speaking softly Mr. Cecola said, 'I promise you your life will be bright and beautiful until eternity.' Winking in a gentle way, seconds later sleeping as if he were a young child again. Every so often twitching like he was having a once in a lifetime dream. Believing soon he will rise above the gates of heaven. Explore a new world of no evil or pain. One beautiful place surrounded by miraculous angels and kind spirits, genuine, spiritual nonliving souls existing above the magical clouds embracing and guarding us. Anna Maria clearly believes her dear mother has always and will be her guardian angel. Never doubting or losing hope for one day they will be near.

Anna Maria's tired eyes continued to guard her father. Overseeing his timeless expressions on his weathered face. Knowing she and others should never leave sight of him, for Antonio may have something up his cannon sleeve. Her mind was racing with ugly thoughts. Wondering how on earth to deplete all bad from her mind. She immediately gleamed. Thinking again about her beautiful mother, Mary Catherine. Anna Maria closed her eyes. Loosely holding her father's hand. Turning towards the hospital window she smiled.

Hail Mary full of grace.

The Lord is with thee.

Blessed art thou among women and blessed is the fruit of thy womb, Jesus

Holy, Mary, Mother of God, for us sinners, now and at the hour of our death,

Amen.

She whispered, 'Thank you, Mom, I love you. I know you can hear me. You always had a way with words and prayer. Bless you, Mom for you are my angel near or far. Please never leave for you give me my strength and will to survive. Soon Daddy will be miles away in your spiritual world. For now, he must survive through pain and agony to give his little girl away in marriage. I want him to see his only daughter wed. Be carried away for my husband will protect and love me for the rest of our lives. God bless you, Mom, and your platonic world. I pray your life is bittersweet, as it was living on Earth. Love and kisses.'

Emotionally drained and mentally exhausted, her body was slowly shutting down. She needed immediate rest. Her eyes no longer were wide open. Latched shut as if someone had just padlocked and glued them together. Fatigue had overtaken her weak body. For now, she remains tranquil near her father's side.

Chapter 22

A slight tap at the door startled Anna Maria. Her heart was beating a mile a minute. Quickly adjusting her frame of mind. Deeply praying her eyes do not come glued to someone she deeply does not want to ever see, Antonio. Her thoughts quickly subsided. A beautiful vision stood calmly. He was stunning in every way, from his piercing blue eyes, to his masculine physique. Smiling as if she had just won the lottery. Saying, 'Gunnar, I love you.'

Tip-toeing his way into her arms whispering, 'I love you. I have missed you tremendously. How is your father? Please tell me some good news.'

She smiled, ,

'Everything is going to be all right. I promise you.'

'What do you mean?'

'Let's take a little walk.'

Arm in arm they strolled through the halls, peacefully, talking and embracing.

'Well, Anna Maria, what is on your mind?'

Joyful tears sparkled on her honeycomb face. 'Gunnar, my father knows all about Antonio and even more then we do. He no longer has a dying wish, but aspiration for us to be happy and wed near his side.

With no hesitation Gunnar flung her high, swinging in circles, saying, 'Yes. I love you. Oh, Anna Maria thank you.'

'No need to thank me. Thank my father.'

'Believe me I will'.'

'I will see you soon. I love you.'

'Where are you going.'

'I promise I will be back as soon as I can. Important business, for the man we want put away needs to be found and immediately disposed of. Mind you, it will all be legal unless your father has already done something else.'

She sighed, 'Oh my God, please tell me this could not be true.'

'Anna Maria take a deep breath and relax. I told you everything is going to be all right.'

Standing still and all alone. Silhouettes of Gunnar's shadow slowly diminish down the eerie and gray halls. Watching and waiting until no formation exists. Moving slowly all composed before entering through the ward door.

Instantly face to face with a man who no longer remains sane.

Holding strong inches from her father's side smiling, 'Anna Maria. I have been worried about you. Where have you been. Come my love say a pray with me.'

Her heart sank. It felt cold. Cold and as dark as a wintery night. Feeling lost, scared and targeted. No words were expressed from her sealed and frantic lips.

'Please Anna Maria I believe your father knows you are here. Patiently waiting he knew well.' Well enough to sense he was unwanted.

Apprehensively she made her way on the opposite side across from Antonio.

'Whispering, 'Is he well?'

Her mind was racing. What should she say? Yes, no or reply as if shall be his last breath.

She softly spoke, 'I really do not know. No vital signs have changed.'

'Anna Maria, I think we need some time together. Far from here'. Kneeling, asking in a brisk way, 'Will you marry me?'

She was beyond stunned. With no hesitation she spoke irately, 'Not now, Antonio, you must go.'

Within seconds Mr. Cecola's vital signs were erratically bouncing from the top of the screen to the bottom. He had heard every word, irate, furious and overwhelmed with disgust, twitched fingers and redness appeared in his face.

Immediately two nurses marched into the room. Not saying a word. Expressing much concern as one nurse in charged harshly spoke if his vital signs did not go back to normal.

Rhythmically his beating heart slowly danced back to normal. Stunning everyone in the room, including the nurses. He half smiled in a way only Anna Maria could perceive.

Water developed in her painful eyes. Realizing her father was listening. What can she do to release Antonio? Numbness, fear and anxiety raged in her overworked and over tired body. She sensed total fear, from the look on Antonio's stormy and hysterical eyes.

Eyeing her with suspicion he spoke, 'Do you really think I am blind? You will marry me. I will own Cecola & Gold. Right now, your father is lying all alone and nearly dead like a complete vegetable.'

Words could not express how alarmed, shocked and overwhelmed Anna Maria was feeling, as if something terribly bad was going to happen.

'Why are you doing this to me?'

'Because I know you love me. They all loved me.'

'But you lied, slaughtered, destroyed and grabbed their hearts and memory.'

'You can think what you want. I do know this. You are the most beautiful woman I have met.'

'You are out of your mind,' feeling scared beyond anything ever before. In her mind, she really knew he was a psychopath. Trying to convince her he loves her and then expressing her father is already a vegetable.

Anna Maria shakily spoke, 'Do you want me or the company?'

With no hesitation he spoke, 'Both. Your father adores me and believes O am the right man for you. We will be married right here, with a priest and your father.'

'No this is not going to happen.'

'Like hell it will.' Grabbing hold of her arm, 'Do not disobey me.'

Cold haunting eyes shocked Anna Maria. She was thinking. How could this be happening.

'Right here near your father. We will wed soon.'

'My father only gave a verbal agreement for us to wed and you to be president.'

'Look at him. He is practically dead. Believe me he will not be seeing or even saying much.'

'I will not marry you!'

'You do not have a choice. I have the power now and you do not. Babe there is no reason for you to get so upset.'

'Do not call me babe. I'm not your showcase trophy'. Viewing her father from the corner of her eye. Apparently sensing he is aware of what is taking place. Feeling sick to her stomach for he may pass at any moment of total despair and anxiety.

She vocalized, not realizing what she had said until it was too late. 'I'm leaving.'

'Like hell you are,' forcefully holding hard against her shoulder.

She wanted to go, but at the last moment thinking he may do something terrible to her dear father. Thank God with much anger he said no.

Her mind was racing. Picking up he receiver just before making a call. He shouted, 'No. No phones.' Grabbing the phone and flinging it on the hard floor. 'What are you doing?'

'Calling an R.N. my father needs care. Look at him.'

'Do not be stupid, Anna Maria.'

Pacing back and forth moments later staring out the window. She faced the hospital parking lot. In total amazement at what she saw. A little hazy, but apparently help was only a step away from any exit door. She half smiled releasing her hand from the window frame and immediately departing near her father's side.

Bending forward, glancing at Antonio preoccupied on his phone. 'Daddy, I promise you everything will be all right.' Tenderly kissing his cheek whispering, 'Assistance is right below us. Be brave and please do not pay any attention to Antonio's cruel words. Help is near.' Leaning upward in the high back chair. Closing her eyes, visions of police squad cars and swat team of men surrounding areas of the building. Praying Antonio does not do anything out of strong anger.

'Anna Maria it is just you and me baby.'

How could he not even think of her dying father? In her mind she knew he was beyond evil and apparently a psychopath with many hidden personalities. Nightmare of all nightmares to even be near such an evil being. A weak person who needs to be taken down, she inhaled deeply.

He continued to guard her with his devious, lying protective eyes. Scoping her out, as if he had a crazy plan of attack. Never leaving the spot he so proudly circles. Speaking in a language that does not exist in her mind, it seems as though he is addressing a plan. Negotiating in code and deliberating into our major conversation.

Chuckling as he stands arrogantly. Glancing at his watch with his dark eyes as each minute ticked by.

Her mind was busy with unsettling thoughts. Obviously, she had no choice, but to play his game. A very dangerous game, but one she truly believes will have her winning from the beginning. Sooner or later she will have won. Trying desperately to remove any fear from her racing heart. To her crackled voice and cold vibes, she has shown. She knew this was not going to be easy, but she had no choice. There really was only one obvious scheme of action. Kiss him with kindness and play him like a player. One ugly dirty role she must pretend to act on quickly. Con him as he did to her family and many other precious women who innocently lost in the end, betrayed and forgotten.

Turning his head, catching a glimpse she kindly smiled. Raising his eyebrow. He deviously winked.

Holding his hand gently. She felt his warm pulse palpitate, rhythmically. He was maintaining his strength well. Long minutes had slowly ticked by. His grueling pain had settled down. Morphine eventually had done its job. Free of misery for now.

Walking towards her he placed his hand on hers saying, 'How are you doing?'

'I'm doing the best I can do. Seeing him like this reminds me of my mother. She also was in excruciating pain as he is. No words can express how my heart hurts.'

He said, 'I'm sorry.'

He was so convincing almost like he really loved Mr. Cecola. She knew better not to listen to his lying words. Remain sincere and always remember to play his game.

Speaking softly, she whispered, 'Antonio where are your parents. Why have you never mentioned them before. Do they linger in your heart?'

The room was so quiet you could hear a pin drop.

'Well,' she said, 'you can be honest with me. I do care.'

Minutes went by which seemed like hours. He eventually opened his sealed lips. 'My parents are deceased.'

'I'm so sorry. I should have never asked.'

He continued on, 'All I had was my mother growing up. She was everything to me, young, beautiful and full of life. She was my life.'

'What happened.' Knowing her question should never have been asked, but her curious mind needed to know.

He paused for the longest time. 'He was a drunk.'

'Who?' she said?

'My father killed her.'

She swallowed hard, no response.

Silence dominated the room, as he paced one section of the room to another.

Anna Maria felt sorry for him, feeling his inner pain. Losing not one, but two parents is a very devastating painful experience, as she clearly knows well.

Minutes slowly sailed by. He spoke abruptly, 'I hate my father.'

One conversation Anna Maria wished had ended before it begun. She said, 'You really do not need to tell me anymore. I really do understand.'

'No, you do not!'

Anger was bursting through his veins. She could clearly tell by the blotches of red penetrating his angry face and raging eyes, unsettled like a spring stormy night.

'My father was no man. A pathetic human being. His only love was his booze and wild nights. My mother was always alone. Only me by her side. Hiding after late hours each night waiting for the raging alcoholic to make his grand entrance. Eventually he would pass out from exhaustion, as we hid behind a secret door in my bedroom closet. He never knew where my mom and I had escaped. He was not smart enough to ever figure out our hiding place. A secret passageway. This was a ritual we both learned to deal with every night of my life, until one turbulent night.'

Eyeing him with moistened tears she was intrigued immediately by his story, as if she were one of the characters in a novel with years of hate and abuse. She could not help herself. Feeling sorry for a man for living one bitter hell of a childhood. No one deserves what he has seen and been through. Especially for being such a young boy, with a miserable past. She had no idea and wished she would never have asked such a deep and disturbing question. This was just the beginning of their conversation. She clearly knew. Understanding now how he became the person he is today. One evil person and a loner. In

Antonio's mind he is the only one who exists on the Earth. In the past, his mother and only her.

Eyeing him she felt his pain.

Looking straight into Anna Maria's eyes he repeated, .My father killed my mother. He was drunk in my mother's car. The car skidded off the road, sailing straight into a telephone pole. She died instantly. My life ended as did hers.'

Unstoppable tears blurred her vision.

Standing still he continued. 'Two policemen came to our front door. I already knew. Closing the door in front of them, with no words spoken. I immediately ran out the back door. Never did I look back. I was numb, lost and lonely. I hid for days. Traveled by train and learned to live on my own. Never did I hear from my father again. He destroyed my life and took away the most important person to me. My precious young mother. She was my world, as I was hers.'

She did not want to ask but felt strong.' Do you know where your father is now?'

He spoke with much anger, 'I hate him,' he shouted. 'Rotting behind bars. If not, he most likely is dead. One raving alcoholic and a pathetic man. He was never a father to me or a good husband to my mother. Hell is where he belongs.'

Walking slowly towards him without any hesitation she reached up and gave him a tender hug. Closing her eyes and seriously wondering if he was telling the truth or if it was another one of his coning lies. She did believe him, from the rage, sorrow in his eyes and from the sound of his crackling voice. She believed the truth has been told. One very disturbing childhood of love, hatred and murder. Having no hope, dreams, just hatred for the whole world.

He lost grip of her walking towards the back of the room.

Eyeing him with much curiosity. She prayed deeply he would not even think about glancing out of the hospital window. The air outside was slowing becoming thick, as total darkness was just minutes away. Closing her tired eyes, glancing upward she silently prayed. Please forgive me all the bad I have done and let this hellish nightmare come to a complete peaceful end. I'm begging you. Antonio's piercing eyes suddenly were glued against the chilled window. Glaring as if he were once again abandoned.

She felt numb, frightened for she knew this was just the beginning of one stormy night. With no hesitation she placed her hand on her father's palm gently squeezing.

Opening one eye he felt her pulse beating a mile a minute. He sensed fear from his darling daughter. Whispering, 'Everything is going to be all right. You need to tough it up and play his game. Whatever it takes to bring him down. Hang in here baby girl be strong.'

She watched her father fight hard to stay awake. Seconds later as usual his tired eyes shut into total darkness. Leaving her once again all alone and with a man who is beyond evil.

She whispered, 'Please, Antonio, stand by my father's side.'

No answer.

'I would really like for you to be near.'

No response.

Turning towards her he glared.

She swallowed hard, 'Are you OK? You look a little concerned.'

Scratching the side of his face he smiled in a mischievous way.

She stood frozen, feeling alone and very much afraid. Praying soon someone captures Antonio and takes him away. Why are the police taking so long? Her father's strength is no longer strong. She knows he does not have much time. Why must this be so difficult.

From the corner of her eye she could clearly see him. He was slowly approaching. No concerned look, as if he was not aware of his surroundings. Men were circling him ever more. Did he really think he would never get caught? In his mind he was too clever for anyone to ever take him prisoner again. He has grown into a man with multiple personalities and too brilliant of a mind to ever get caught again.

She gently kissed her father's cheek. Whispering, 'Daddy, I love you.'

Whispering in her ear he said, 'I love you. Anna Maria.'

Fighting hard to hold back her tears. She could not resist. Tiny teardrops cascaded down her chilled cheeks. Tears of fear and not sorrow.

With the tip of his fingers, Antonio gently wiped each wet tear away. Saying, 'I believe everything is going to be OK. If you do not love me now. You will grow to admire and deeply love me. I always treat my ladies with respect. You are by far the fairest of them all. Soon we will wed and have the happiest marriage one can create. Your father knows what is best for you'. He smiled, reaching for her hand.

She felt ill to her stomach, as if she were going to faint. She said, 'I need air.'

No words or response from him.

She had no choice, but to walk over and open the hospital window. Deeply breathing in the chilled air, she immediately felt like a new person. She no longer felt weak, fatigued or sick. On the other hand, glancing down towards the parking lot she grew alarmed. Men were everywhere, pointing many forms of firearms directly her way. Playing it smart. She gently closed the window and made her way towards her father's side.

Antonio spoke sincerely, 'Do you feel better?'

'Thank you, yes. I really do not know what just got into me. I suddenly felt like I was going to pass out.'

'You are stressed. You really need some time away. I will make some plans for you.'

'Please, Antonio, I will be fine. My father needs me right now. In the future I will get away. To a beautiful place and that holds deep in my heart.'

He eyed her curiously, 'Where might that be?

She half smiled, 'I will never tell.'

He really did not know what to think. Why is she not telling him? Curiosity triggered his eyes. She clearly could tell. It was apparent he had no idea what she was talking about. Which made him a little disturbed and edgy. What was he going to do or say? Was he just going to let this conversation just slide by?

Changing the conversation quickly she said, 'I pray my father forgives all who have done him wrong.'

His mind was racing. She could tell.

Antonio spoke, 'What do you mean by that?'

Her plan had worked. Listen to the old and wise in return get what you want. Remembering her father's words. Which he had just spoken earlier. Play his game. The game called cat and mouse. The loser shall rot in hell and it certainly was not going to be her.

Again, he asked, 'Why did you say you hope your father forgives all who have done bad to him?'

She smiled, 'I do love my father, but he is a very powerful man. He holds grudges and I do not think he has ever depleted grudges from his mind. I pray he forgives all before his eyes close forever.'

Her words truly bothered him. His boggling mind was bouncing in every direction.

She had just won. No more words. Just total silence filled the room, as if the calm before the storm.

Chapter 24

Half asleep slightly daydreaming and awakened from a repeating tap on the hospital door. Her eyes opened. Where is Antonio. She grew alarmed. First seeing if her father was all right. Then walking towards the door. Her mind was deeply racing with terrible thoughts. Should she open the door or remain barricaded, but she was no longer haunted by Antonio's presence. Where did he go? Had he escaped or walked away and headed into total madness. Swallowing hard slowly pushing the handle down she smiled.

'Gunnar, I accidently fell asleep and when I woke up Antonio was gone. I'm scared. I have no idea where he is. You need to find him.'

Smiling he whispered, 'Anna Maria, believe me. He can no longer run and hide. It is all over.'

'What do you mean?'

'Right about now, he is most likely behind steel bars.'

She looked puzzled. 'What are you talking about?'

'While you slept, Antonio for some reason left the room and within seconds he was handcuffed and taken away.'

'You are kidding, right?'

'No, Anna Maria, I truly believe in his mind he did no wrong and would never get caught. It was apparent he had no idea the feds where after him or even us for that matter. It was as if Antonio did not exist, but another man with a different personality. Walking around the hall corner. A few officers cornered him. With no fight he was handcuffed, read his rights and taken away. The whole ordeal was quick and seemed so simple.'

Tears streamed down her face.' I love you.'

Speaking from the heart he said, 'You know, Anna Maria, I almost think he wanted to get caught. Why else would he act so strange?'

'Remember he is a very sick man. See he has your mind wandering. He will play games during his interrogation and try to fool them all. He will no longer win, for the professionals have all the information they will ever need. Our life is complete, for we now can move on.'

He watched her curiously.

She asked, 'Do you really think he will ever harm us again?'

'Why do you ask.'

'I'm just worried. He is good at what he does. One good con artist and it is hard to believe he is gone from our lives.'

He half smiled, 'You should have seen the look on his face when they handcuffed him. He truly was stunned and unprepared for his arrest. Men were everywhere, as if a bomb was ready to go off. Many innocent people were waiting for this day for a very long time now.'

'Gunnar,' Mr. Cecola echoed softly, 'come please.' He whispered, 'With all my heart, thank you. I'm truly grateful to have you in my life. You are blessed into this family and to be a Cecola.' He reached for his hand. 'I would love to have you as my son in law. I'm deeply sorry for all I put you through, especially my daughter. She did not deserve all the pain. Please make up all the hurt I have ever endured.'

He listened, wide open eyes, sealed lips, closely hearing his cherishing words.

Mr. Cecola desperately inhaled,' I'm truly sorry. Sorry I never took time to get to know you. Take care of my baby girl. She deserves the best.'

Fighting back the tears he smiled, 'I love your daughter very much. Mr. Cecola, I promise you Anna Maria will be happy the rest of her life.'

Holding strong, clutching his palm, 'I do have one request.'

Gunnar looked concerned. 'Yes, what is it?' Turning his face towards Anna Maria.

'Please, my son, live in the mansion and do not desert Rosie.'

He swallowed hard, 'Thank you.' Slightly squeezing his hand, he smirked,. 'Rosie will fly above the gates of Heaven and will be a saint. She will be carried away and blessed by all. All who have known her love her dearly. I will always remember her as a beautiful caring human being. I promise she will receive her dying wish.'

Anna Maria as well as her father had a curious look in their blinking eyes. No words were expressed, for they both had secrets sealed within their warm hearts. No need to ask questions, for time is slowly ticking by.

Gunnar leaned over Mr. Cecola whispering with a glow in his eyes, 'You will also receive your wish, be patient, rest your tired eyes and when you awake. You will hardly believe what you see. Remember one thing. I did this all for you. I know your heart can be cold, but tomorrow it will flutter warm.'

He arched his eyebrows, half smiling, 'I will see you tomorrow.' Within seconds darkness filled his closed eyes.

Anna Maria hesitated, 'What is so special about tomorrow?'

'You will see. It will be magical and a monumental day. Filled with love.'

She smiled, 'My father does admire you. You may not believe so, but I do. His heart is no longer cold, but pain free and warm. I just pray he stays with us a little longer, so you two can create a bond, tenderness.'

'Time is slim, for he loves you deeply. In his mind he knew there was a slight chance Mr. Cecola's eyes would not reopen, but he had to believe in faith. He only had to hold on a few more agonising hour. Then may God bless his soul and sail his spirit above the golden gates of Heaven.

Chapter 25

Alone, nervous, breathless with an extraordinary view, she remained hidden in the corner. Eyeing everyone from her resting room. Beautiful fresh red bouquet roses were placed throughout the entire room, with a trace of white lace. The room was small, but beautiful in every way. Peace and warmth filled everyone's hearts. She felt more alive today than ever. With each tender beat, her heart fluttered to the sounds of soft music echoing in the background. Her favorite instrument, the harp.

A gentle tap startled her. Glancing down he looked so charming, with a smile that captured her heart.

She inhaled deeply, 'Daddy, thank you.'

'Anna Maria you are more than beautiful, an angel.' Reaching his hand towards her he smiled. He whispered, 'I do believe your time has arrived. Please we must move along.'

Hand in hand she stood beautifully tall. He sat patiently near her side. Just before the music began, he recited, 'Honey, I do love you. You have made me very proud. Please forgive me.'

'Daddy I love you. No need to worry, for you gave me the best gift of all.'

'No, my love you gave me the most precious gift. A new son in law to walk my one and only daughter down to the altar. Excuse me not walk, but wheel you down the altar.'

She giggled, 'Oh Daddy thank you. Gunnar has always been the one for me. I will make you proud and run the most successful company in the Midwest Cecola & Gold.'

He replied softly with tears in his eyes, 'I know you will. I never ever doubted you. Now let's go to business.'

She took a deep breath. Closing her eyes for a few minutes and taking in all the beauty that surrounds her. Eyeing everyone, it's not the grand cathedral all Cecola's marry in, but a quaint little chapel located in the center of her father's hospital. No church bells ringing, altar boys, or mass amount of people. Just a small wedding with close friends and family. Certainly not the wedding she has always imagined. How could she think different? What was important to her and Gunnar was having her father near her side.

Glancing up towards her he asked, 'Are you happy? I'm so sorry you just found out about your wedding day bright and early this morning. Gunnar and of course our dear lady friend Rosie spent many hours planning this day.'

She smiled, 'I love it, thank you.'

Suddenly, music from the harp intensified, sending chills down her spine. At the same moment they turned towards each other and smiled. She walked slowly, as he pushed the wheelchair with one hand between the small pews, before coming to a complete stop.

Gunnar looked amazing with his black tailored suit, matching pressed shirt, red tie and a beautiful smile that never came to an end. She looked just amazing with her long flowing hair gently pinned up, lightly fresh makeup, with a hint of shiny pink gloss on her tiny lips. Her mother would be proud, for she wears her dress well. Fitted perfectly thanks to Rosie. White modern wedding dress with just a touch of lace flittering down the center of her back, her mother's veil, long and worn to the ground.

Struggling hard to stand he gave his very own daughter away. A gentle kiss and a wink to the groom. No more words. Just a calm heart, as tiny tears streamed down his cheeks.

One charming priest. Very young, energetic, humorous and excited to marry Gunnar and Anna Maria. His first quote. He was thrilled to wed the first Cecola, as his uncles have wed many. Ending with, 'I bless this wedding with all my heart. You may kiss the bride.'

Sounds of people clapping echoed throughout the tiny chapel, as they exited for the door. Gunnar gave an honest smile, as a total stranger opened the door for him and his new bride. Gunnar shook his hand, as a puzzled look appeared on Anna Maria's face. He said I believe this is a quote from Rosie. Her true words. I just want to see his face just one more time.

Anna Maria or Rosie could not believe their eyes, it was Robert. They stood for the longest time just taking it all in. Tears streamed down Rosie's pale cheeks. She said, 'You came back.'

He spoke openly, 'Yes.'

One step out the church doors. A shooting star had appeared. Laughing while looking at Gunnar. She knew this star well. The most beautiful one ever, her mother. Looking towards the shining star she spoke softly, 'Thank you. Mom you will always remain in my heart. She then turned towards her father she smiled. Minutes later he closed his tired eyes into total darkness, for there is no more pain.

9 781837 940844